DEATHWATCH

DANA MARTON

First Edition: 2013
Updated Edition: 2020
ISBN: 9781940627472

This book is a work of fiction. Names, characters, places and incidents are products of the author's imagination or are used fictitiously. Any resemblance to actual events or locales or persons, living or dead, is entirely coincidental.

DEDICATION

My sincere thanks to Diane Flindt for midwifing this book, to the amazing Sarah Jordan for having my back. Deathwatch couldn't have been born without the support of my family and friends who graciously put up with all my craziness. And a HUGE thank you to my exceptional readers. I enjoy few things more than spending time with you on Facebook. Thank you for answering all my questions!

Returning from war, all Murph wants is the solitude of his house. Except, when he arrives home in the middle of the night, he finds a beautiful stranger sleeping in his bed.

"I read my first book by Dana Marton yesterday, my second one this morning, and this, my third one, this evening." (Ann De Vries, about DEATHTRAP)

"Marton has raised the bar! Her books just keep getting better, and this one with Bing and Sophie will have you cheering, laughing, crying and sighing. Loved it!" (Denise McDonald, about DEATHTRAP)

"Dana Marton's books are just as enjoyable to read as Nora Roberts's romantic suspense books, and I look forward to all future books that Dana writes." (Donper98, online review for DEATHWISH)

CHAPTER ONE

Kate Bridges thought attending her own funeral would be the hardest part.

She barely breathed inside the FBI van as she watched the live footage from a dozen hidden cameras, and listened to the clear notes of "Amazing Grace" floating from the organ.

Her family and closest friends filled up the first pew. Her mother sat wedged between Kate's father and sister, clutching her black pashmina scarf around her shoulders. The chapel always stayed cool, although the California sun radiated merciless heat on the Spanish-style church on the outskirts of Los Angeles.

The images on the FBI monitors were grainy but the audio perfect, catching even the softest sobs of grief. The heartrending sound stabbed Kate in the middle of her chest.

"This is a mistake." She sprung from her chair, the sudden movement bringing inevitable pain. "I can't." She gritted her teeth. "Nobody should have to go through this. I want to tell them now."

The forty-something agent next to her shot her a sharp look, her eyes the color of gunmetal. Everything about the woman was no-nonsense, all business, down to her short black hair and meticulous charcoal suit, paired with black sneakers meant for running. "In a little while."

Tension sizzled between them for an interminable moment, then Kate lowered herself back into the chair, but only because the way Cirelli was watching her said the agent would tackle Kate if she tried to leave.

Inside the chapel, the stout priest behind the coffin was encouraging the grieving family to accept God's will. "We cannot hope to know the mind of our Heavenly Father, but his mercy is everlasting…"

Kate believed in that mercy with all her heart. After all, she was alive. She rubbed her fingertips over the uneven rows of her handknit Christmas sweater, not what the average person would pick for a funeral in July, but if she ever needed her lucky sweater, this was the time.

Between the sweater and the figure-eight brace she wore to stabilize her broken collarbone, she looked a sight. She was in rough shape, but not rough enough, thank God, for a funeral.

Since having to watch her family grieve her was killing her, she glanced at the monitors that showed the outside of the church and the parking lot. "Where is the hearse?"

"In the back."

She found the right monitor, nothing back there but the black Cadillac that waited for its sad cargo, and empty asphalt.

In contrast, the front parking lot was crowded with family sedans and SUVs. The two flower delivery vans stood toward the front. The real Ferrone's Flowers van carried funeral wreaths. Its twin, the covert FBI vehicle parked a hundred feet away, did not. To a casual observer, the two white vans would look identical, down to the pink roses painted on their sides. Nobody would suspect the double row of monitors and the two women the FBI van hid inside.

"How much longer?" Kate tugged at the neckline of her sweater. The space was too small for all the equipment it held, claustrophobic. Like a coffin. Like being buried alive.

Cirelli, a hand on her earpiece, didn't respond. She focused on information coming in from the rest of her team. They all reported in at regular intervals.

Kate couldn't hear them, but the audio from the chapel continued through the monitors loud and clear, filling the van.

"In this time of despair, beloved," the priest said, "let us remember..."

Kate kept scanning the mourners as she'd been told, until the wax replica of herself in the white coffin drew her gaze again. A shiver ran down her spine, disjointed thoughts racing through her brain. "Do you think the dummy looks real?"

Agent Cirelli tapped her earpiece, muting her mike. "They put on plenty of makeup. The face is a little off, but it's what people would expect after a car crash."

Probably true, the head-on collision with the tree had been brutal. That part hadn't been faked. Kate had a broken collarbone to prove it—in addition to a myriad of cuts and abrasions that covered her upper body, courtesy of the shattered windshield.

What her family and friends inside the chapel didn't know was that the crash hadn't been a random accident. She'd driven into that live oak because her car window had been shot out, the bullet whizzing by within an inch of her face.

"Let us turn to God for comfort," the priest encouraged, while Kate tried to remember in vain what had happened immediately after she'd hit that tree.

She couldn't recall the ride to the hospital either. She'd been mostly unconscious, according to the paramedics. That she'd looked dead from afar had probably saved her life. If she'd as much as twitched while firefighters dragged her from the wreck, her would-be murderer might have taken the risk and squeezed off a second bullet.

To keep her safe, the FBI had decided to leave her

'dead' for the moment. So her family was at her funeral, while the FBI was trying to trap her killer—the whole plot as far-fetched as a Hollywood movie. She'd had no idea, until now, that stakeouts like this happened in real life.

Kate shifted in her seat and kept watching the screens. Maybe, like most Hollywood movies, the day would come to a happy ending.

The agent next to her tapped off. For a split second, something that might have been sympathy filled her eyes. "Shouldn't be long now. He'll come, we'll grab him, then you can tell your family why we had to do this. They'll understand. You're doing the right thing here."

"I hope so." And, honestly, what other choice did she have? "I suppose this is what happens when you're the only person who can identify the most wanted hit man in the country."

"It's our first real break since we've been looking for Rauch Asael," Cirelli said. "Before you popped up, we had little more than his list of aliases and his hit list. We appreciate your cooperation."

The agent didn't even pretend to care that Marcos was dead. For the FBI, the world was divided into *bad guys* and *good guys*, along very firm lines. For Cirelli, Marcos would have been listed on the *bad* side—no sympathy, good riddance. While Kate had nightmares of him choking on his own blood and dying in her arms.

Marcos had been her first true friend, one of the few people who stood up for her when they'd been two lost kids in foster care. He'd been one of the smartest people she knew, loyal, and kind—which he'd tried hard to hide.

Cirelli tilted her head, the blue of the monitors reflecting in her eyes. "If you have any information about Marcos Santiago's businesses—"

"I don't." How many times were they going to ask? "Marcos never talked to me about business. He knew I didn't approve. I wanted more for him. He would have been successful at anything he tried. He *was* about to be successful. Big time."

He'd been trying to change, start new, do better. *Too late.*

"Anything you can tell us about him could be helpful. Look, we got his rival who ordered the hit. You want the hit man brought to justice too, right?"

Kate scanned the monitors. "That's why I'm here."

She'd seen the bastard's face as he'd been slinking away from his dying victim. But while the FBI hadn't been able to find the man based on the image their sketch artist had drawn from her description, Asael had no trouble tracking down Kate.

She glanced at Cirelli. "Do you think he'll come?"

"You're the only person who can make positive ID."

Translation: the killer needed to make sure she was dead. He couldn't afford to let Kate live.

Her aching muscles clenched harder in her shoulders, her throat dry and tight. Nervous energy buzzed through her, urging her to her feet, but the rigged-out van had no room to pace. She hugged herself, her gaze drawn back to the monitors, to her white coffin smothered in a blanket of pink and white roses.

Her mother still saw her as someone perfect and innocent. She'd always seen Kate as a pure soul, never as someone tainted by past abuse and a rough time in the system. She saw Kate as more than the insolent preteen the social workers had dropped off in the middle of one night with her toddler sister, more than the wild cat who threw food on the floor and punched holes in the walls when she couldn't control her pain and anger.

"How did you meet Marcos Santiago?" the agent asked.

"I already told the officers who responded to the 911 call the night of the murder, and then again to the agents who came to see me once the FBI became involved." No doubt, Cirelli had it written down somewhere, word for word, in a fat file.

"Tell me, anyway."

Fine. The agent thought of Marcos as nothing but a hardened criminal, and that wasn't right. Marcos had stood up for Kate time after time. Kate owed him a testimonial.

"We were in the foster system together, had a short-term placement with the same family once. He defended me on a bad night, was sent to a group home for it. As we both got kicked around the system, we'd end up at the same school now and then. For some reason, he got the idea that he was responsible for me. We lost touch for a year or two, met up again in high school."

Her gaze cut to her family on the screen. "I was with new people by then, being loved and taken care of." Despite her sea of mistrust and prickly personality. "Marcos wasn't that lucky. He came to school with bruises more often than not." She'd seen them, no matter how hard he'd tried to hide the black-and-blue welts that covered his skinny legs and arms.

"He was dealing by then, everything from pot to other kids' ADD meds. He didn't use." That would have been a waste and stupid, according to Marcos. "He was in it for the money. He wanted his independence more than he wanted air to breathe. He wanted to be in a position where nobody had power over him ever again."

The agent nodded. Maybe she could relate to that, at least.

"Here is the truth, the only difference between us…" Kate held the woman's gaze. "The world treats little white girls differently than it treats little black boys."

Cirelli didn't comment on that. Instead, she said, "You kept up with each other over the years."

"Barely. After high school, I went to UC Santa Cruz, and he moved to LA. We'd lose touch for months at a time, then he'd call in the middle of the night when he was in the mood for a stroll down memory lane."

"He fancied himself as your protector."

"He *was* my protector. More than once. When he

found out that a boyfriend hit me, then stalked me after I broke up with him, Marcos visited me at college."

Cirelli's eyebrows arched. "The ex-boyfriend switched schools the next day?"

He had. "We didn't talk much for a while after that. Marcos was busy with other things."

"How did you hook up again?"

"My father was transferred to the LA headquarters of his company, so we moved. I ran into Marcos at a party."

He told her he'd sold off some of his shady businesses, was making a slow shift toward becoming legit, producing music. "He just bought a penthouse apartment in the middle of the city. With a doorman. He was so proud of it. He invited me up for drinks. He said that in exchange for having some outstanding charges dropped against him, he was turning evidence on an old rival." She shot a dark look at Cirelli. "The FBI promised him protection."

"That night he invited you over… Was that the night he was killed?"

Kate hugged herself tighter as she nodded.

When it became clear she wasn't going to reveal anything further, Agent Cirelli held out a business card for her. "If you ever remember anything about the people Santiago worked with, I'd appreciate a call. I understand that he was a friend. I understand that he had good in him. There usually is, in everyone. But he worked with some seriously scary associates, and if we could get any of those guys off the streets, everyone would benefit."

Kate took the card, shoved it into her back pocket without promising anything, then they both refocused on the memorial service, although they'd kept their eyes on the monitors even while they'd been talking.

"Would you like a sandwich?" Cirelli poked the white takeout bag hanging from the back of her chair.

Kate shook her head, even if turning down a meal went against her instincts.

Her earliest memory was hunger. Food made her feel

safe. Sometimes, if she didn't pay attention, she hoarded groceries.

She never forgot how after a day without food, hunger woke with soft growls, not very threatening at all, maybe like a cat that sat heavily on your stomach. After two days, the dull pain came. The stomach cramps didn't start until the third day. But when the woman who'd given birth to her left Kate locked in the filthy one-bedroom apartment for a week at a time, hunger roared like a tiger, clawing her small body, threatening to eat her from the inside. She could remember begging for food as soon as the front door opened. When she had, the woman beat her.

The woman. The monster. Kate never thought of her as her mother or used any expression to refer to her that included the word.

The first foster home she could remember was the Pereiras when she'd been around four or five. The Pereiras had food in the refrigerator all the time. They didn't hit; they were churchy people. Kate had her first piece of chocolate after a children's service at church, and forever associated chocolate with heaven, and with everything good and right.

Her time with the Pereiras didn't last long. Too soon, she had to go back to the monster. Beyond the hunger, Kate most remembered the beatings and the shouting.

I'm gonna snap your neck, you little shit.

Shut up or I'll stomp your stupid guts out.

I'm gonna smack you so hard, your head will snap off, you hear?

All delivered from the screaming, wild-eyed face of death.

By the time Kate was ten years old—the woman all big and even moodier because she'd forgotten to rid herself of her latest pregnancy in time—Kate had been threatened with violent death a million times. And she *believed* she would die.

She was small, weak, and hungry, while the monster was strong and all-powerful. Kate *knew* she would die—starved or beaten to death—it'd be a matter of time.

Impending death had been her closest childhood companion. Yet, watching her own memorial service now, more than two decades later, was still beyond surreal.

The priest continued the eulogy in the chapel, his shock of black hair a contrast to his pristine white robes on the grainy monitor. "The length of our lives has little to do with the impact we make, and this has certainly been true with Kate."

Kate blinked her burning eyes. Her family should not have to go through this. She hated every minute. She'd only agreed to the deception because she would hate it worse if her loved ones were hurt because of her. Emma could have been in the car with her when that bullet crashed through the window.

"Although she is gone from among us…" The priest went on.

Emma, a decade younger than Kate, lowered her head, her long black hair cascading down her shoulders in waves, nothing like Kate's short, blond pixie cut. They had different fathers.

The priest began to pray.

"Are you going to make them go to the cemetery?" Kate asked Cirelli.

The agent swallowed the last bite of her sandwich. "Things shouldn't come to that. Asael will put in an appearance here, before the coffin is closed."

Of course. He would want to make sure Kate was inside. Then the FBI would grab him, and all the pretending could end. As mad as Kate's family would be at her for this setup, she hoped they'd be so happy that she was alive that they would forgive her.

When she'd agreed to this miserable charade, she hadn't thought it would ever get this far. A break-in at the funeral home had been anticipated; the FBI kept the "body" under constant surveillance. But in the end, it seemed the killer was going to take the easy way and come to the chapel, slipping in among family and friends.

The priest wrapped up his brief closing prayer. "We ask you this in the name of our Lord, Jesus Christ. Amen."

Kate shivered. The air conditioner in the van was cranked to the max. As ridiculous as her lucky Christmas sweater—a gift from Emma—looked in July, she was glad she'd brought it. Even if Emma had miscounted the rows so the reindeer's left hind leg was a little bent and a little high, making him look like he was happy to see Mrs. Reindeer.

Agent Cirelli leaned closer to the monitors. "Do you see him?"

The longer they waited, the more the agent's shoulders tightened. She was going to need a massage to work the knots out, Kate thought and scanned the pews again, looking for the face that haunted her dreams. A few seconds passed, the bitter taste of disappointment bubbling up her throat. "I don't think he came."

Inside the chapel, Emma stood up and walked slowly to the coffin. Her shoulders slumped into a tired angle, hurt etching her face. She looked more somber than a teenager should ever have to look, shaking her head as she stopped behind the microphone, her big brown eyes brimming with tears. "The strange thing is that I don't feel like Kate is gone. I don't feel it in my heart."

Kate blinked in unison with her, wanting more than anything to break out of the van, bust into that chapel and shout, *I'm here! This is all a big mistake.*

She glanced sideways at Cirelli who said, "Almost over."

Emma, standing close enough to the coffin to lay a hand on it, cleared her throat. "My first memory of Kate is when I talked her into helping me set a trap for the tooth fairy. I was six, just lost my first tooth."

God, the tooth fairy incident. She remembered that? Tears flooded Kate's eyes at the same time as a smile tugged at her lips. She pressed her fingers to her mouth as her sister gave a greatly embellished version of the story.

As Emma recounted their mad caper, their father slumped farther down in his seat. Their mother laid her head on his shoulder, pressing a tissue to her eyes. An invisible fist squeezed Kate's heart.

She had to be the most heartless person in the universe to let them go through all the grief.

Or a woman without a choice.

Sam Roecker, Kate's business partner, said a few words next, his face drawn.

"That's the coworker, right?" Cirelli asked. "He does rehabilitative massage too?"

Kate nodded. "One of the people who developed it."

A special form of therapeutic massage for abused children who might never have been touched in a way that didn't hurt, kids who feared physical contact.

When Kate had knocked on his door for a job six years ago, knowing what she'd wanted to do but not how to go about it, he'd hired her, then trained her.

She'd missed her job this past week, wondered about her patients, worried about them, even though she knew Sam would take good care of them. "He's a good friend. The best therapist I know. He's—"

A movement on the nearest monitor caught her attention—a man about the right height easing in through the side door, stopping just inside. He wore black shoes, black suit, black tie. Nothing about him drew attention. He looked the same as all the other men in the chapel. Yet the breath Kate was about to take lodged in her throat, her heart lurching into a desperate rhythm. Cold sweat beaded on her forehead.

The man's posture was apologetic, as if embarrassed for being late. His nose was wrong, and the hair color too, but that jaw…

The jaw was right.

CHAPTER TWO

Agent Cirelli pointed at the screen. "That one?"

Kate nodded, instantly back in Marcos's penthouse apartment again, blood all over the white rug, bubbling up Marcos's throat, coating her hands as she hung on to him and begged him to live.

Cirelli tapped her earpiece. "We have visual confirmation in the chapel. I repeat, we have visual confirmation."

Then she snapped out orders to the team of undercover agents on standby. On the screen, two mourners stood in the back pew. A member of the chapel choir stepped away from the rest.

Kate's entire body stiffened as the killer stood up, slid out of his pew and slowly moved toward the side door.

He wouldn't get far. Undercover agents were blocking the exits.

He glanced up as he reached the door, staring into the camera hidden in the flowers. His cold eyes blazed through the display screen in the van.

I'm coming for you. The look on his face sent the message

as clearly as if he had spoken.

Even as Kate gasped, the man slipped through the door and disappeared from the monitor. A handful of "mourners" followed him.

"We got him." Agent Cirelli stopped the live feed and rewound the footage, freezing it on the killer's face for a closer look. Endless seconds ticked by as she listened to her earpiece.

Heart pounding, Kate clutched her hands tightly on her lap, telling herself to breathe.

Almost over. Almost over. Just another minute.

She waited for Cirelli to say *all clear.* Instead, all hell broke loose in the van.

"Two agents down!" Cirelli was a blur of motion as she jumped to her feet and checked her weapon. She leaped to the door. "You stay here." And then she was gone, the door slamming closed behind her.

What?

"Hey!" Kate held her breath, expecting the agent to reappear for a second, with the bare minimum of explanations, at least, a sentence—but Cirelli didn't come back.

No, no, no, no. Kate gripped the armrest of her chair as she turned to the surveillance monitors where her memorial service eerily continued. *What happened?*

She wanted to watch her family, make sure they were safe, but the frozen monitor grabbed her gaze, mesmerized her, wouldn't let her look at anything else.

The killer stared right at her, as if he knew exactly where she was. A cold chill ran down her spine. She rubbed her arms.

They'll get him. The trap was foolproof; the FBI had promised. Everything was still going according to plan. Cirelli had said they wouldn't grab him in the chapel to make sure none of her family got hurt, but they had a tight net in place. He'd have no way to leave the church. *They'll get him, for sure.*

Mindful of her broken collarbone, Kate maneuvered her way to the black curtain that separated the back of the van from the front seats, opened the panels an inch, and peered through the gap.

The double doors of the church, carved with solemn angels, stood closed, the front steps, always crowded before service, empty at the moment. Not a soul outside, until an old woman shuffled through the metal door of one of the emergency exits, her Sunday hat covering most of her face.

Her back slightly hunched, she made her way carefully forward. She slowed by the real flower delivery van and bent down as if adjusting her shoe. She straightened and hurried forward much faster a moment later, then she ducked between two cars with a sudden agility that belied her age.

When the flower van exploded the next second, the earth shook. Car alarms went off all around, loud enough for Kate to hear, despite the surveillance van's soundproof paneling.

The old woman popped up behind her cover then hurried toward the FBI vehicle.

Asael. She had to be.

Kate kept her head down as she lunged to the front seat, ignoring her injuries, awash in adrenaline. *Hurry!*

Fingers trembling, she opened the door on the side away from the killer, just wide enough that she could slide to the ground, never popping so high that she could be seen through the window. She closed the door and rolled under the car next to the van, her shoulder screaming with pain. She kept moving anyway. She crawled under the next vehicle, then the next and the next, gritting her teeth.

Pain or no pain, she couldn't afford to stop. Any damage she caused would be negligible in comparison to the damage Asael could do to her. *Go, go, go!*

She had no idea how far she'd made it before the second explosion hit, shaking the ground under her and spraying her with fine gravel. Dust covered her face, sticking to sweat. She had to blink several times before she finally cleared the muck from her watering eyes, which was only partial improvement. She still had dirt in her nose, in her mouth, in her lungs. She pressed her lips together and refused to cough, no matter how hard her chest spasmed.

She couldn't hear footsteps over the ringing in her ears, but through the settling dust she could see a pair of black shoes rapidly approaching, the feet way too large for an old woman. She watched the killer break into a dash, and she prayed she wasn't hiding under the man's car. Then he was right there suddenly, coming straight toward her.

Run!

The command her brain issued translated into nothing more than a second of lame flailing. She was too bruised and battered to flee. So she reached for a fist-size stone by her hip, even as she knew it wouldn't make a difference. As soon as Asael backed his car out of its spot, he would see her on the pavement. He couldn't possibly miss her. He couldn't possibly leave her. He would pull his gun and end his troubles with a single bullet. Kate gripped her makeshift weapon anyway. If this was it, she wanted to go out swinging.

Muscles wound, she was ready, but Asael ducked into the next car over. And a blink later he was gone, peeling out of there as if he was at the racetrack.

Thank you, God. Kate coughed at last, spit dirt, coughed again. She lay staring up at the filthy undercarriage, the rock rolling from her limp fingers. Seconds ticked by before she gathered herself enough to crawl from under the car, gritting her teeth against the pain in her shoulder.

People were spilling from the church in panic, her family among them. Shock joined grief on her mother's face. Her father had his arm around her, holding her up on one side, Emma supporting her on the other.

Kate's body shook as she fought the overwhelming urge to run to them.

I'm here! I'm here! I'm here, she screamed, but only in her head.

Her lips stayed pressed together while she watched, hidden by the fire and smoke of the burning vans, as the agents herded everyone back inside so they could secure the parking lot.

Cirelli was circling the destroyed FBI van, gesturing wildly with her arms, her mouth moving. She looked to be shouting, although, Kate couldn't hear a word.

She shook her head in vain to clear the ringing from her ears. She needed to lean against something for a second to catch her breath. The lid of the trunk moved under her hand. The explosion must have popped it open.

Common sense said she should head back to the agents. Reality said they couldn't protect her. They hadn't been able to protect Marcos, and Marcos had been just a job for the killer. Eliminating Kate was a lot more personal.

If Asael saw her…he would keep coming until he killed her. He couldn't afford to let her live. And if he came after her, her family could easily become collateral damage, caught up in the crossfire.

Kate's overwhelmed brain struggled to think, circling back to the same thought over and over: the only way to keep her family and herself safe was to disappear forever. So instead of running toward the church and the FBI, she opened the trunk and scrambled awkwardly inside, pulling the lid closed with her good arm.

Hidden. Safe. She coughed again then wiped her face with her sleeve. *Breathe.*

Except for the faint glow of the emergency-release lever, darkness surrounded her. The trunk smelled like rubber from the spare tire in the tire well under her. Her knees pulled to her chest, the cramped space reminded her of the gap behind the washing machine in the laundry closet where, as a kid, she used to hide from the monster's hard slaps. Some people disliked tight, dark places, but Kate thought of them as sanctuaries.

She closed her eyes. *He didn't get me.* She was alive. And once she was far away, the people she loved would also be safe.

The image of her family running from the church—their red-rimmed eyes and the shock on their faces—would not leave Kate's mind. God, she was going to miss them. Tears gathered. She blinked them back.

The first and only place she'd truly felt protected and safe was with the Bridges. For her, they defined "home" and "family," the two things she craved above all else. After today, she would no longer have either.

Kate's breath hitched. The tears won at last.

Fire trucks wailed in the distance, coming closer and closer. Agents shouted orders in the parking lot. She could see little in the dark trunk but she could finally hear again.

She didn't know how much time passed before someone came for the car she'd chosen for her hiding place. The driver-side door opened, then slammed shut. The engine hummed to life. Her head swum. She was about ready to pass out from the heat. Compared to the air-conditioned FBI van, the trunk was an oven.

The car rolled a little as the driver took his foot off the break. Kate's fingers curled into tight fists, her nails sinking into the heels of her hands. Her entire body tensed. Panic surged through her anew, stealing her breath.

Oh God.

She could still pop the trunk from the inside with the emergency lever. She could reveal herself.

The car backed out, then turned and slowly rolled forward, away from her family. Tears washed down Kate's dirty, sweaty face. The invisible hand that had been squeezing her heart all day squeezed with renewed strength. Merciless.

She had thought attending her own funeral would be the hardest part. She'd been wrong.

Leaving it was harder by far.

CHAPTER THREE

Broslin, Pennsylvania
18 Months Later

"Murph! Dude, wake your ass up."

Murphy Dolan shifted drowsily on the passenger seat as he woke, every limb stiff after the long flight from Germany to Philly, then the ride from the airport. He blinked his eyes open, registering the dark interior of the car first, then the fact that Tommy, his Army buddy, was pulling up the driveway.

God, the house was a welcome sight.

"See?" Tommy nodded at the clock on the dashboard that showed 2:00 a.m. "Told you it'd be a quick drive. No traffic in the middle of the night." He peered bleary-eyed through the windshield, leaning his forearms on the steering wheel. "Nice digs."

Home. After an eight-month deployment in Afghanistan, Murph's semi-renovated Victorian with its peeling paint and dark windows was the most beautiful thing he'd ever seen. For the first time in a long time, his battered body relaxed. "It'll be nicer when I fix it up."

He craved the quiet solitude of his house, the peace and normalcy of the Pennsylvania small town he called home, and the safe sanity of everyday life.

"Not bad for the backwoods is what I'm saying." Tommy looked up and down the street. "Like living in a Christmas postcard."

An inch or so of snow covered everything, the moon hung huge in the sky, bathing the houses and trees in silver light. Maybe the town did look like a postcard. Broslin was a place you'd want to come home to, the kind of place where people knew and watched out for each other. Murph couldn't imagine living anywhere else, but to each his own. "Wilmington has its own charm."

"Dude, city girls." Tommy offered a sleepy smile. "Bright lights, big titties."

Murph shook his head as he stepped into the cool night air, then grabbed his Army duffel bag from the back of the SUV they'd rented at the Philly airport. He'd fronted the money, and Tommy drove, since the shrapnel in Murph's left shoulder still hurt too much to be hanging on to the steering wheel for long.

"What?" Tommy asked. "You're not excited about girls?"

"Right now, all I want to do is go back to sleep. In my own bed, in my own house."

"Then what?"

"After I sleep for about a week, I'll see about finishing the house." Then, eventually, back to work. He was going to reclaim his old pre-deployment life and never leave town again. "Want to grab a cup of coffee?"

Tommy rubbed his eyes with the back of his hand. "My parents are waiting up." He flashed a dopey smile. "My mama's probably standing by the window."

Murph nodded, his gaze sliding to the house next to his on the left. The FOR SALE OR RENT sign was gone, a single light on in an upstairs window. Looked like he had new neighbors.

Good. Abandoned houses in a neighborhood drew crime.

On his other side, Mrs. Baker's house slept, dark and quiet. She spent winters with her grandkids in Florida since her arthritis couldn't take cold and snow.

In the morning, before he drove his pickup over to the PD to talk to his boss, Murph would walk around her place, make sure everything was all right.

"Damn bleak," Tommy said, "coming home to an empty house. How about I take you with me for a hot meal, at least? Taste my mama's cooking. I could drive you back here tomorrow."

"I'll be all right. Thanks. And thanks for the ride."

Tommy waved off Murph's gratitude, as if saying the small favor was nothing. They'd been brothers on the battlefield, had stood back to back in a field of bodies.

"Hope I see you around," he said. "You'll miss the Reserves. Admit it, if the doc didn't kick you out over that shoulder, in a month, you'd be standing at the end of the driveway, waiting for me, ready to go back to training."

God's honest truth, Murph thought. "Listen, stop in sometime. All right? I'll keep a six-pack for you in the fridge. And until then, stay out of trouble."

"What are the chances of that?" Tommy grinned and backed down the driveway.

Murph watched the car disappear at the end of the street, then he filled his lungs with cold air and headed for his front door, dead on his feet. He'd been traveling nonstop the past two days, since he'd been released from the field hospital in Bagram, Afghanistan.

He dropped his bag in the small foyer, then locked the door behind him, untying his boots and kicking them off as he went, shedding clothes on the floor. Plenty of moonlight filtered in the windows, so he didn't turn on the lights, a decision he regretted a moment later when he stubbed his toe on the sofa. *Dammit.*

Looked like his brother had moved around some of

the furniture. Of course, he did.

Doug had asked to stay a week when his wife had tossed him out in the fall. He'd ended up staying a month and a half. Murph hadn't minded. No sense in the house standing empty.

He would drag the sofa back to the window later. All he wanted right then was to stretch out his weary bones and sleep on his own sheets. The renovations weren't finished, the upstairs pretty much a construction zone, but the big downstairs master suite was fixed up. *Thank God for small mercies.* Kitchen and living room too. Everything he needed. He'd have time now to complete the rest, little by little.

Down to nothing but his ACU pants, Murph dragged his tired, aching frame into his bedroom, then pulled up short.

What the hell?

He blinked at the nearly naked woman in his bed, but she didn't disappear.

Her long legs lay tangled in the sheets, her mess of reddish-brown hair half across her face. Her white nightgown, nothing but a scrap of fabric, looked shrink-wrapped around her torso and hips. He caught her scent, a faint trace of old-fashioned roses, sexy and somehow homey at the same time.

Okay.

He stared, suddenly wide awake and then some. *Better than okay.*

As a welcome-home present, he approved 100 percent.

Except for the screaming.

* * *

Kate dreamt of a shadow chasing her, catching up, closer and closer, ready to kill her. Even as she ran, she knew it was a dream, a familiar nightmare returning to torture her over and over again. *Wake up!* she ordered herself as she ran.

Then she woke, but not to an empty bedroom as always before. This time, she saw the shadow of the killer at the end of her bed and screamed. Then she yanked her weapon from under her pillow, flipped the safety off, and aimed at the bastard.

This was *not* how she was going to die. Not here. Not today.

His hands shot right up. "Take it easy, sweetheart."

The voice—deep, relaxed, and sexy—wasn't what she'd expected from the country's most dangerous hit man. The timber didn't match the coldness she'd seen in the man's eyes at her funeral; she could detect no ruthlessness in the tone.

A shaft of moonlight glazed his body, outlining an impressive amount of muscles. He seemed unarmed. And mostly undressed. Unexpected, in a number of ways, but here, definitely here.

Let me be still dreaming.

She'd dreamed of him finding her a million times.

Except, this wasn't a dream. This time, the fear and the rush of blood in her ears were all too real. *Okay, then.* She regulated her rapid, shallow breathing with effort. Her brain needed oxygen. She'd prepared for this. He hadn't caught her completely unaware. She was ready.

"I want to see your weapon," she demanded when she found her voice. "Throw it down."

"I'm unarmed."

Right. His weapon was probably hidden behind his back, tucked into his waistband.

"Don't move." She'd been holding the gun with both hands but now reached for the phone on the nightstand with her left. She had 911 on speed dial. She pushed the button but didn't try to pick up the phone. She couldn't afford to be distracted. The call itself should bring a patrol car to the address.

She had this all thought out, had imagined it over and over. She had prepared.

"You might be the better shot, but I have my gun out and aimed," she warned the intruder, even if words would never hold back a man like him.

She braced herself for an attack, to respond in a split second. She couldn't hesitate. She had to shoot the moment he moved. *Oh God, it's happening.* Her worst nightmare. Right now.

He tilted his head and looked her over, took his time. "You belong to Doug?"

Her frenetic mind struggled to make sense of the question. "No."

"I don't suppose I could talk you into putting that gun down?"

"Doug who?"

"My brother. I'm Murph. He probably told you about me. This is my house."

"No, it's not. It's mine. I'm renting." At least for a little longer. She never stayed in one place long, no matter how much she wanted to stop running.

"From?"

"Doug Dolan." *That Doug?* Dammit, her brain needed to wake up all the way.

The man in her bedroom swore under his breath. "Doug's my brother. I didn't know he rented out the house. It's not his to rent." His impressive shoulders rose as he filled his lungs. "I'm going to reach out very slowly and turn on the light. All right?"

She hesitated only a moment before nodding. "The better I see, the better I can shoot you if you try anything."

She squinted so the light wouldn't blind her, but even so, when he flipped the switch and light flooded the sparsely furnished room, she had to blink a few times.

She looked at nothing but the intruder. Wrong height—this one was several inches taller than Asael. Wrong shape—his shoulders were much wider. Wrong chin—although that could be faked with a facial prosthetic. But the overall body couldn't. As good as Asael was, he couldn't have grown over the past year and a half. Which meant Kate had the wrong guy at the end of her weapon.

Regardless, she didn't lower the gun. He might not be

the killer she was running from, but he *was* the man who'd broken into her house, into her bedroom, half-naked in the middle of the night. She kept her arms steady.

He drew his dark eyebrows together. "I was deployed overseas. I landed back stateside a couple of hours ago. Murphy Dolan. Homeowner. I swear."

His camouflage pants and the dog tags hanging from his neck matched his story, but Kate was still shaking inside and not nearly ready to trust him. "I want to see your ID."

"Out in my bag by the front door." He paused as he watched her. "How long have you been living here?"

"Six weeks." Which meant she had another four and a half months left on her short-term lease. Then she would move again.

She'd been scouting places already, a small lake community down in Maryland in particular, but hadn't found a house yet. She didn't like apartments. She couldn't be stuck up on the third floor of a building. She needed multiple emergency exits.

He stepped back. "I'm going to back away now and grab you that ID."

"Turn around first. Slowly."

He raised an eyebrow but complied.

He had no weapons on him, hadn't been lying about that. He did sport some major scars, however, fresh ones, on his left shoulder and side. And when he turned back to her, she noticed that his left arm didn't move in sync with the rest of his body.

Since he, supposedly, was coming home from war, she guessed an IED. Or he could be lying, fresh out of prison, the scars reminders of a nasty cafeteria fight.

"All right. Let's see that ID." She slid out of bed to follow him. No way was she going to let him out of her sight.

He flicked on lights as he went. She noted the trail of clothes on the hardwood floor in the hallway, then the duffel bag that stood where he'd said it would be, next to the small hall table that held her keys and the junk mail. He reached into the bag, rifled around for a few seconds and pulled out a beat-up wallet, held it open for her.

She inched closer, tightening her fingers on the gun. "No sudden movements."

"You're the boss." His tone remained calm. "No worries. I get it. I'm not going to try anything."

He seemed even bigger up close and personal. It'd been a long time since she'd had a semi-naked man within arm's reach. Awareness skittered across her skin. Regardless, she focused on what she needed to be doing here.

She inspected his driver's license and military ID. The address matched, and so did his picture, a younger version, but definitely him, *Murphy Dolan.* He wasn't the hit man who was hunting Kate, and it didn't look like he was some serial killer slash rapist fresh out of prison either.

She backed into the kitchen, collapsed into the nearest chair, then laid the gun on the table as her hands began shaking. "I'm sorry. You scared me."

"No harm done. You didn't shoot." His lips twisted into a wry smile.

"I could have." Her stomach clenched. She could have killed an innocent man.

"Chances were slim. You're not a professional, and you don't look like some gung-ho hothead. Professionals shoot before the target has time to think about it. Hothead amateurs shoot before *they* have time to think. You gave me time to explain myself."

He crooked a dark eyebrow. "On the other hand, if I meant to harm you, you'd be dead. Something to remember when you're in trouble for real. Don't give 'em a chance to get you."

He might have said more, but the sound of sirens cut him off, a police cruiser flying up the street.

Dammit, dammit, dammit.

The thought of having to deal with an officer of the

law made cold sweat bead on Kate's back. She'd jumped the gun on calling the police. *No cops* was her rule to live by. Her fake driver's license, obtained when she'd posed as a student and lived in a college dorm for two months, would not stand up to scrutiny.

"I did rent this place from your brother. I swear."

"How do you know Doug?"

"Met him at Finnegan's." Broslin's Irish pub. "He overhead me asking the bartender about an available place."

He'd offered the house, and she paid in cash the next day. The price was right, and Doug wasn't the type to insist on credit checks and references, or formal contracts for that matter.

Kate didn't want to have to move and deal with another landlord, so she looked her middle-of-the-night intruder in the eye, and said, "I recently started a new job in town. I'm definitely going to need to keep this place."

"We'll talk about that in a minute." Murphy Dolan stepped into his boots. "I'll be right back." Then he walked outside, all muscle and power like some medieval warrior, heaven help her.

If Murph challenged her lease… Without a rental agreement, if Doug couldn't be found or decided not to back up her story, she was nothing but a squatter. She could be arrested for breaking and entering. And if the police ran a background check on her, she'd be so busted.

She dug into the fruit bowl on the table and pulled a small foil packet of chocolate from the bottom. She unwrapped it and popped it into her mouth. One, if eating chocolate at two o'clock in the morning was wrong, she didn't want to be right. Two, emergencies were emergencies.

Keep hiding, stay alive had been working for her so far. The FBI was hunting Asael. One day the agents would catch up with him, or someone else would. A professional assassin had to have a few enemies. Once Asael was eliminated, Kate could return home to her family. All she had to do was keep running until then, trust no one and let no one find out her secret.

The cruiser pulling up the driveway turned off its lights and siren. She hurried over to the window but couldn't see through the windshield past the headlights, couldn't tell who had responded to the call. She knew a few of the officers by sight, from the diner. Still, that they tipped her didn't mean they wouldn't prosecute her. She couldn't afford to be entered into the system. It wouldn't have surprised her if Asael had access to the police databases.

Kate's instincts screamed to pack and run. Her heart drummed fast then faster. Her feet moved, without a conscious decision on her part, toward the bedroom that held her meager belongings and her scuffed suitcase.

She could disappear through the back while the men out front were distracted.

CHAPTER FOUR

"Captain." Murph stepped off the porch as his boss unfolded from the cruiser at the top of the driveway.

Ethan Bing strode up the snowy brick path for a handshake and a good thumping on Murph's back. "When did you get home?" His gaze dipped to the scars on Murph's shoulder. "You all right?"

They were about the same height, used to be same body type too, but Murph had bulked up in the Army, while Bing had lost weight since their last meeting. He looked haggard; the smile on his face—as sincere as it was—didn't reach his shadowed eyes. Bleak darkness clung to him, as it clung to soldiers after the bloodiest battles.

Murph didn't like that look. "Got in five minutes ago. Everything okay at the station?"

Bing stood in hard silence for a moment, then his shoulders collapsed. His strength went right out of him: the light in his eyes, his smile, his spirit. It was like watching a controlled demolition of some high rise. "Stacy was killed." The words came out in a hard, brittle tone. "Three weeks ago."

Shock plowed into Murph, a blast from a hand

grenade. He barely felt the cold. "What the hell happened?"

He'd met Bing's wife a couple of times, although she rarely came to the station. She was an overworked corporate manager with little extra time.

"Home invasion gone wrong." The muscles in Bing's face tightened with undisguised pain. "I was out on a call."

"Any leads?"

Bing shook his head, his thoughts written on his face. *I'm supposed to protect the town, and I can't even protect my own family.*

His presence at Murph's house suddenly made more sense. As captain, he didn't have to work the night shift. But maybe it was easier for him to keep busy than being home alone at night. He sounded destroyed, stricken. Eaten up with guilt.

"What can I do?" Murph asked.

Broslin PD was a tight team. They backed each other up. They were there for each other.

Bing shook his head. "We're already doing everything that can be done. Followed every damn lead. Turned over every rock we could think of. Got nowhere. It's as if the bastard disappeared into thin air." He glanced toward the house. "What can I do for you here?"

"Sorry about that." Murph winced. "My brother rented the place out. I scared the tenant."

"Doug didn't know you were coming home?"

"I wasn't sure until the last minute," Murph told Bing, just as his *tenant* stepped outside.

"Kate." Bing's expression lightened. "I didn't know you lived here."

"Captain Bing." She wrapped her slim arms around herself against the cold, staying in the shadows of the front porch. She radiated nerves, shifting from one foot to the other. "I'm sorry about the call. I'm okay."

She had a slight accent Murph couldn't place and didn't think long about. Plenty of other things to notice about her. Her long legs and wild curves drew a man's eyes, and so did her skimpy nightgown that had 100% of his approval. She redefined sexy.

In the cold night air, her nipples puckered, visible under the material even in the semidarkness of the porch. Her scars didn't show out here, but he'd seen them under the harsh kitchen lights. She had as many as he did, although hers were older, pale white.

Bing didn't seem to notice her state of undress. He glanced back to Murph to see what he wanted done.

"We're good," Murph said as Kate pulled back into the house. "How do you know her?"

"New waitress at the diner. Nice young woman."

Maybe. Except for the gun she'd held on Murph.

The radio went off in the cruiser, someone reporting suspicious activity in the main parking lot at Broslin Square, and the captain turned back that way for a second as he listened. "Whole county's on high alert for the Tractor Trio Gang."

"Tractor what?" Maybe Murph had been gone too long. Nothing was making sense.

Bing groaned. "They pick out a bank, then drive a stolen tractor or other farm machinery through the glass in the front. While everyone screams and runs, they grab the money, then disappear in a getaway car. Two men, one woman, farm-animal masks. The woman drives the tractor."

Murph rubbed a hand over his face as he tried to picture all that. A farm-themed robbery. *Only in Broslin.* And yet… He looked at Bing. "Honestly? That sounds kind of fun."

He wouldn't have minded investigating the case.

The everyday, crazy quirkiness of police work was blessedly normal compared to what his life had been overseas, leading good men deep into enemy territory to ferret out insurgents—no backup, no quick way out, staring death in the face every day and hoping you wouldn't blink.

He nodded at the town with his head. "I missed this."

Bing backed toward his cruiser as his radio kept going.

"You're welcome to jump right back into the fray. But you need some rest first. I'll talk to you tomorrow. Go inside before you catch a cold."

Murph looked after the man as he drove away.

Stacy's dead. Bing's wife. Freaking killed.

His brain was too tired to fully comprehend it. The senselessness of the tragedy pissed him off, made him want to punch something. Bing needed help. And Murph wasn't coming back to work, not for a long time, not until his shoulder healed. As he was now, he'd never pass the physical. He already hated the conversation they were going to have to have about that.

He hated to feel useless. He wanted to be there for his captain and the rest of his team. PT was the answer, as soon as possible. *But first,* he looked toward his house, *I need to deal with the problem at hand.*

What were the chances that his pinup-girl tenant would be reasonable, take a refund check on the rent and leave him in peace, pack up and go to a hotel?

"Probably none," he muttered under his breath. With looks like hers, she was probably used to getting whatever she wanted. Murph headed inside, ready to introduce her to disappointment.

A dark sedan pulled away from the curb down the street, catching his eye.

He paused.

Nobody had walked up to that car while he'd been outside. Which meant whoever was driving it slowly in the opposite direction now had been sitting behind the wheel all this time. In the middle of a cold winter night.

Murph didn't like how that happened, where the car had sat without headlights. The hesitant way it was moving away pricked his instincts honed on searching for IEDs. You saw a certain type of car, a certain time of the day, in a certain spot, and you learned that bad shit followed.

People blown to bits.

For a second, he saw the blood and heard the screams,

and he had to clench his jaw till it hurt to make the images stop.

"I'm home," he said the words out loud to remind his brain.

The car didn't mean anything. He was back home in Broslin, not in Afghanistan. He needed to focus on the problems he faced right here, right now, namely the redhead who'd somehow come between him and his bed.

His mind jumped to an image of the two of them in bed *together.*

If he wasn't so exhausted, he would have laughed at himself. He was no better than a sailor on shore leave. The faster he rid himself of the temptation she presented, the better. Murph cursed under his breath as he opened the door and caught sight of her. He was definitely putting some clothes on her before they started negotiating the terms of her lease.

CHAPTER FIVE

Why, why, why did he have to show up now? Kate watched as Murphy Dolan stalked through her—okay, technical *his*—living room. He was looking around as if cataloguing the place. He picked up the worn blanket that had come with the couch.

"I didn't steal anything," She snapped from behind the kitchen island, second-guessing her decision to stay rather than to leave.

He ignored her. Of course, he did. He was a soldier used to being in command. He was probably used to having the upper hand in any given situation.

Not tonight. Not if she had anything to do with it. Step one was to firmly establish the fact that she was *staying*. "I can drop you off at a hotel, if you'd like."

"I'm not going to a hotel."

"Neither am I."

These days, every place required ID. And every time Kate had to show hers, she risked that someone would spot that it was fake. Also, she didn't have the kind of cash she would need to live in a hotel until she found another rental where they wouldn't scrutinize her and her background overly much. She needed a place that didn't require a credit check and references, and they were few and far between.

"I have a valid lease on this place."

Her landlord tossed her the blanket. "It's chilly in here."

She lay the damn thing on the counter. "I like it a little colder at night. Helps me sleep."

He shot her a dark glare as he strode to the sink for a drink of water, his stride slightly off. *Sore right hip.* Probably another battle injury.

He drank, then set his empty glass on the counter, his eyes—the color of the finest dark chocolate—never leaving her. "I didn't catch your full name."

She hadn't given it. "Katherine Concord. Everybody calls me Kate."

He rolled his neck, then leaned against the counter as he watched her. He had to be exhausted. Maybe she could use that to her advantage.

"Can we talk about this tomorrow? I pulled a double shift at the diner today." Angie's daughter had a fever, so she hadn't been able to come in. "Eight hours of running around and serving meals is tough. Sixteen is murder." She played for sympathy. "I'm dead on my feet."

She wanted time to think, away from him, a chance for her brain to settle and start fully working without a half-naked warrior staring at her. She was too tired and frazzled to match wits with him tonight. She needed to be on her toes for that, negotiate well and give none of her secrets away.

He rubbed a hand over his face. "Fine. Is my pickup still in the garage?"

The attached garage held *a* truck. She nodded. "I thought it was Doug's."

"I'll sleep in the pickup. We'll figure things out after I have a chance to call my brother in the morning." Murph pushed away from the counter, picked up the blanket, then headed for his duffel bag by the door, and picked it up.

"Where's all my stuff?"

"I didn't remove anything. I just shifted things around. Doug said it was okay to rearrange the furniture."

"I meant my clothes."

She shrugged. "I saw boxes in the basement. I don't know what's in them. I don't go down there much."

His mouth tightened.

Go, go, go.

No. She couldn't be this selfish.

She wanted nothing more than for him to leave so she could have the place to herself again, but he was a soldier back from war, injured. She couldn't make him sleep in the freezing garage.

He seemed like a decent guy. She didn't think he'd attack her while she slept. The bedroom door had a lock. She had her gun.

"Wait," she called after him as he turned away.

She wrapped her arms around herself. Establishing some goodwill between them might help her with their negotiations in the morning. "Why don't you sleep on the couch?"

His eyes searched her face. "Are you sure?"

"Not really, but I'm going to go with it anyway. I can trust you, right?"

"You have my word." His frank, straight gaze held hers. "I'm an officer of the law here, by the way, when I'm not overseas. Broslin PD."

Wasn't he a delight?

A cop-soldier surprise landlord. She needed him like she needed a fork in the eye.

Kate picked up her gun from the counter. "Okay. I'll talk to you in the morning."

By then, she would come up with a foolproof plan to make him go away. She had the night to figure out how to talk him into yielding ground and letting her stay.

She walked past him and down the hallway without looking back, locked the bedroom door behind her and went straight to bed, leaving the loaded weapon within easy reach on the nightstand.

She sighed as she closed her eyes, beyond exhausted, weary to the bone. Within seconds, she was out.

She woke what seemed five minutes later, to the sounds of someone moving around in the kitchen, and had her gun in hand by the time she remembered the man she was suddenly sharing a house with. *Murphy Dolan.*

The light of dawn streamed in the window. The next second, her alarm went off, blaring. She slapped at it. She'd fallen asleep without producing a brilliant plan to deal with Murph. *Great.*

"Welcome to another fun-filled day," she muttered under her breath as she looked up at the ceiling.

Murph *Freaking* Dolan.

The only people she liked less than social workers were police officers. She hadn't trusted them as a kid, and she didn't trust them now. They'd never protected her.

Back when she'd lived with the woman who'd given birth to her, if the neighbors had heard screams or seen her beaten up, they called the cops. The cops called the social workers and handed her over. The police never held her abuser long enough. The woman would get out of jail, pretend to turn her life around, and then the social workers would give Kate right back to her. The beatings would start all over again.

Kate drew a deep breath and shook off the lingering anger and sadness. "Rule Number One: Don't borrow trouble from the past."

Her life would be what she made it. And she would make it great—as soon as Asael was caught, and she could go back home. The past wasn't going to define her. She refused to allow it.

Her brain and body begged for more sleep, but she slipped out of bed and went to the bathroom, washed her face, brushed her teeth, pulled her hair into a tight ponytail—all without looking into the mirror. Even after all this time, she still felt like she was looking at a stranger, every time she caught a glimpse of herself. After she'd gone into hiding, she'd picked a dark auburn color with a fair amount of red and let her hair grow below her shoulders, the opposite of the beach-blond pixie cut of her previous life.

She'd changed her clothing too, her style. Her colorful California shorts and tank tops had given way to neutral colors and denim, suburban-housewife capris in the summer. She shaped her eyebrows to change their angle, and used eyeliner to change the shape of her eyes. She'd put on five pounds to change the shape of her body, and wouldn't have minded another five.

As she turned away from the sink, she caught an unintentional glimpse of herself anyway.

"Ah, dammit."

The thin material of her nightgown showed a clear outline of her body.

Her sleepwear had been selected for its small size and light weight, a convenience for packing since she moved a lot. She hadn't planned on anyone seeing her in the flimsy piece.

She winced at the thought of having walked around in front of Murphy Dolan practically naked.

Maybe he hadn't noticed.

And if he had… She closed her eyes for a second. She had bigger things to worry about this morning.

Forget last night. Get dressed. Get to work.

She hurried back to the bedroom and yanked on her uniform—tan skirt, white top—then checked the FBI's home page on her tablet, her usual morning ritual.

She stared at Rauch Asael's image on the Most Wanted page for a second, the grainy photo taken at her funeral service. They hadn't caught him yet. If they had, he'd be off the list. She swallowed her disappointment and shut off the tablet.

"I will go home soon," she spoke the words to put the

universe on notice.

One day, the killer's picture would be gone from the wanted list, the man finally in custody. Then Kate could cook with her mother again, tease her father about not letting anyone ride his lawnmower, and listen to Emma talk about boys with all the drama of a teenager.

Except, of course, Emma was no longer a teen. She was almost twenty-one. Kate blinked. *Fudge.* She'd missed too much. S*o damn freaking unfair.*

And then there was Murph. What if she was unable to talk him into leaving? He wasn't going to be intimidated by her or any argument she might muster. He hadn't been intimidated when she'd held a gun on him.

You catch more flies with sugar than with vinegar, her mother, her *real* mother who'd actually raised her, used to say. And her mother was usually right.

Kate hurried out to the kitchen, flashing a confident smile. "Hi."

Murph was sitting at the kitchen table, staring at a cup of coffee as if he was about to interrogate it, wearing camouflage cargo pants and a standard-issue Army T-shirt. The overhead lights glinted off his biceps and chiseled forearms.

Okay. Wow. Now that it wasn't the middle of the night and Kate wasn't scared to death, she could acknowledge that her landlord was ridiculously hot. A minor distraction she was certainly adult enough to overcome.

"Good morning." She widened her smile. "I hope you slept well. How about I make you something to eat?" She flitted into the kitchen, full of take-charge energy, and snuck a square of caramel dark chocolate from the utensil drawer.

He turned a bleary eye on her and grunted.

Great. He was in a bad mood. He couldn't be in a bad mood when they were about to have a discussion that would have a huge effect on her life.

Kate popped the chocolate into her mouth.

Cheer him up. Quick. She turned on the radio, and her

favorite pop-rock station blared to life. He might have grunted again. She couldn't hear it over the music. She wanted another square of chocolate but resisted.

His biceps flexed as he lifted the mug to his mouth. The olive-drab T-shirt stretched over his wide shoulders. A twenty-four-hour shadow emphasized his masculine jaw and— *Stop ogling him!*

"How about bacon and eggs?" She hurried to the fridge. "With pancakes."

She had to be able to stay.

"Orange juice?" She poured a tall glass and set it on the table in front of him, then went around him to the cupboard for flour, accidentally bumping against his shoulder in the small space.

She hopped back, stubbed her toe on a chair, saw stars, but gritted her teeth and did not let her smile slip.

She was going to hold on to that damn smile if it killed her. *Positive, positive, positive.* She glanced toward the window, out into the dreary winter morning. "I think we're going to have a beautiful day."

* * *

What now? Murph grunted as he stared at Miss Chirpy's bare feet. Her toes, tipped with orange polish, looked like ladybugs marching on his dark slate kitchen tile as she walked and talked. If she didn't quit, they were going to have to discuss duct tape.

A man needed time to wake up, and at least two cups of coffee, before being confronted with that kind of happy-peppy energy.

He tuned her out as he raised his gaze, little by little. *Long legs.* Her skirt hid precious little of them. His gaze moved higher. The way her soft cotton shirt outlined her breasts…okay, that eased his pain a little.

The basic male, caveman-Murph wanted nothing more than to roll back into his bed with her and celebrate his homecoming long and hard. Every time he looked at her, his mind dropped straight into the gutter. He drew another sip of his coffee, hoping it'd facilitate his return to sanity.

"Want chocolate chips in your pancakes?" She danced by him, smiling like a demented pep-rally queen.

Okay, nobody was *that* cheerful. What was wrong with her?

"No, thanks." He couldn't afford to fall into a sugar coma. He had a busy day ahead of him—first item on his list being moving her out of his house.

He stood with his mug in hand, the Broslin PD logo comfortingly familiar and sane, walked over to the radio and turned it off. "I thought maybe we could talk."

She kept the smile, but she had to work at it.

He refilled his coffee. "So, you waitress at the diner?"

She nodded as she lay strips of bacon into the skillet. Then she grabbed the bag of bread on the counter. "How about toast?"

Murph nodded. "What brings you to Broslin?"

She dropped slices of bread into the slots, smacked the lever down, then hurried to the fridge. "How many eggs? Scrambled? Sometimes I make them poached. It's no trouble."

"Scrambled is fine. Thanks."

Those little ladybugs were ready to fly away, she zipped around Murph's kitchen so fast.

He sipped his coffee as he watched her, then set his mug down on the butcher-block counter of the kitchen island he'd installed himself. "How about you tell me how much money you paid Doug? I can refund it. I'll even help you pack. Obviously, now that I'm home, the house is no longer available."

Her hand jerked as she cracked an egg, spilling some on the side of the bowl. She kept smiling, but her muscles were tight around her eyes, her shoulders drawn in.

She was acting like a woman scared, and he didn't think she was scared of him in particular. At first, yes, but not any longer.

Her forced smile widened, a distinct air of desperation

about her as she asked, "Are you sure there's no way I could stay? Doug promised six months. I was really counting on this. Mr. Dolan—"

"Call me Murph. I can help you find another place. Bing owns a couple of rentals. He's a friend of mine. I can call him for you."

"No!" She nearly dropped the fork she was using to beat the eggs into oblivion. "No," she repeated a shade calmer, then caught herself and set down the fork. "Thanks."

Scared of the police?

Murph tried to imagine what she could have done to send her running from the law. Maybe nothing. She looked too damn innocent by half, the type who'd turn herself in if she jaywalked.

When she paused here and there and thought he wasn't watching her, her sparkling blue eyes turned into sad angel eyes the color of the winter sky. Her shirt hid most of her scars on her chest and upper arms, but he hadn't forgotten them from last night. She could be running from someone other than the law. That dark sedan from last night sprung to mind.

Murph finished his coffee and set the empty mug in the stainless-steel sink next to her. "Where did you live before moving here? You got any family in Broslin?"

She didn't look at him. She turned the bacon in the skillet instead. "How many pancakes do you think you'll eat?"

She avoided personal questions like a champ, like she'd had practice. *Scared Woman with Secrets*—Murph had seen this movie before, many times. It featured a man in the picture somewhere, a real gem.

"No pancakes. Bacon and eggs will be fine." Murph rolled his shoulders. He had a special contempt for men who beat up women.

He hoped he was wrong about her and that wasn't her story. But if it was?

"I'll take a shower while you get breakfast ready." He walked away from her and could swear he could sense her deflate behind him as the tension left her body.

He picked up his shaving kit from his duffel then walked down the hallway that cut the house in half.

The only working shower was in the master bath, which was accessible only through the master bedroom. Who would rent a house under construction? *Nobody, unless they were desperate.*

He opened his closet and stared at Kate's skimpy selection of women's clothing for a second. *Right.* His clothes were in the basement. She'd told him that.

He plodded back down the hallway, turned on the basement light and drummed down the steps, then shook his head as he took in the haphazard pile of boxes Doug had clearly rescued from the liquor-store dumpster.

"The more things change, the more they stay the same," Murph muttered under his breath as he grabbed the nearest one, the side advertising cheap whiskey, and found a jumble of underwear and socks. He set the box on the bottom stair, then kept looking until he found his T-shirts and finally his jeans, then his old leather jacket.

After he carried his boxes upstairs, he took a quick shower, with soap that smelled like roses. He found one of his own gray towels in the back of the linen closet so he didn't have to borrow any of Kate's. She had only three.

The glass shelf under the mirror wasn't filled with tubs of creams. She had a small bottle of body lotion, a comb, toothbrush, toothpaste and not much beyond that. Like her clothes, her toiletries were sparse and nothing fancy, nothing that couldn't be tossed into a suitcase at a moment's notice.

Murph brushed his teeth then shaved, then he ambled back into the kitchen.

The mouthwatering aromas of bacon and fresh coffee floated on the air, the room bathed in the warm glow of the overhead lights, definitely a contrast to the gray winter morning outside. Especially with Kate in the middle of it all.

She smiled when she noticed him, wiping her hands on a dishcloth. "Hey, ready to eat?"

Some unnamed emotion hit Murph in the chest, and he stared for a second. This was *The Dream*, wasn't it? Most lonely men in the Army wanted to come home to something like this: a beautiful woman in the kitchen, cooking food for you with a smile on her face.

Except, it had never been *his* dream. He preferred living alone, actually. He had a stressful job. What time it left him, he spent with the Reserves. When he was home, he wanted solitude and peace.

And none of the current warmth and companionship was real, anyway. Kate wasn't here for *him*. And she wouldn't stay.

She couldn't stay. He didn't want her to stay. Why did he have to remind himself of that all of a sudden?

Murph frowned as he strode to his chair. "Thank you, Kate."

"No problem." She hovered in place instead of grabbing a plate for herself. "I hope you like it."

"Aren't you going to eat?"

"I'll have something at work." She wrung her hands, then dropped them at her sides, and forced another chirpy smile. "If you could stay with your brother—"

"Not an option." He cut her off before she could run too far with that fantasy.

Doug's wife, Felicia, wasn't a fan of visiting relatives. She wasn't a fan of Doug either, really. Doug crashed on Murph's living room couch pretty frequently.

Kate glanced at the clock on the microwave. "I have to leave for work. Maybe we can talk when I come home later?"

Maybe she thought she could put off the discussion until he forgot about it, or even long enough for her to stay out her lease. Did she think he was stupid?

Murph shook his head. "You going to tell me what

you're so scared of?"

Her shoulders immediately snapped straight, a tough-chick expression coming over her face—sexy as hell, even if she was faking it. Or maybe because of that. He found the contrast in her, between the woman she really was and who she wanted him to think she was, fascinating.

Her chin came up. "I'm not afraid of anything."

"Which is why you sleep with a loaded gun."

"It's not much use unloaded."

He had to give her that. "If you're in trouble, maybe I could help."

"No, thanks. Please don't talk yourself into some great mystery here. I'm a small-town waitress who's renting your house. End of story. If you're looking for intrigue, I'm sure you can find some at work."

All right, so she put him in his place. Fine. Rescuing damsels in distress wasn't in Murph's short-term plans anyway. And she might not be a damsel in distress. For all he knew, she was a bank robber on the lam. Maybe she belonged in handcuffs. The thought brought a few interesting images to mind. Murph cut them off as she walked away from him, but he could not stop himself from watching her walk away.

He'd come home for peace and quiet. But as Murph sipped his coffee and looked through the steam, he had a strong premonition that ship had already sailed, been set on fire by pirates, and sunk into the sea.

* * *

Kate dragged on socks and her white work sneakers, shrugged into her coat, then grabbed her purse on her way out. She'd gained time. She considered that a win. The two of them having a talk this afternoon was better than him putting her stuff out on the front porch right at that second. She could think while she was at work today, come up with a winning strategy.

"Don't worry about the dishes. I'll take care of them when I come home," she called back from the door. She wanted him to like her enough to let her keep the lease. And that meant she couldn't snap at him again for asking questions, she couldn't lose it. *Smiles and compliments all the way.* "Don't forget to rest. You deserve it. Have a great day!"

She pulled her twelve-year-old green Chevy out of the double garage, banging on the dashboard a few times in hopes of making the broken heater work. She was so busy with that and worrying about Murph, she didn't notice the man in the dark sedan parked farther down the street.

CHAPTER SIX

"Man, being back is nice," Murph said aloud in his kitchen and drew a slow breath while he tried to consciously appreciate the moment. The doc who'd discharged him recommended the practice. Might as well give it shot while he had the house to himself, his very inconvenient tenant out of his hair.

He shrugged into his winter jacket, ignoring his throbbing shoulder, and walked outside, around the house, scanning the property to make sure nothing needed his attention. He was itching to run a background check on Kate Concord, but first he wanted to see his place in daylight.

He had a half-acre lot, large for the middle of town. Most other properties like his had been subdivided long before.

Every once in a while, he thought about doing the same. He could keep a quarter acre, sell the rest for someone else to build on. The money could pay for the rest of the renovations on his house. But he liked his privacy, liked that nobody was living in his backyard.

Truth was, he was attached to all that space, even if he

had little beyond the garage but grass and a few trees, now covered in snow, and a dilapidated barn in the far corner. The old building stood empty, but the previous owner had used it as a workshop, and it still had two decent workbenches against the back wall, which Murph thought could come in handy. Maybe someday he'd get a hobby.

The yard looked all right. The storms hadn't pushed over any trees; the snow hadn't broken any major branches. Good. He had enough on his to-do list already. Not that he minded work. The thought of putzing around the house with a tool belt made him happy.

He walked over to Mrs. Baker's rancher and checked her place too. No storm damage, no sign that anyone had been around. Since everything seemed fine, Murph returned to his own backyard.

A young woman in jeans and a ski jacket was waving at him from the back deck of the house on his other side.

He waved back. "Hi."

"Hey. I'm your new neighbor." She beamed. "Wendy White."

"Murph Dolan."

"I know. I heard all about you from Doug. Welcome home. Thank you for your service!"

"Uh, yeah. Sure." Murph wiped his hands on his pants, trying for a smile and not quite succeeding as he walked to the back door of the garage. "I'll see you around."

He was no small-town hero, and he didn't want to be one. The people who patted him on the back for being a soldier—starting right at the Philly airport—didn't know the things he'd done and the things that had been done to him.

He tapped the snow off his boots and stepped inside the garage that was the same as he'd left it: summer tires in the corner, toolboxes lined up against the wall. His lawnmower, broken, but it could wait. Spring was months away.

He climbed into his pickup and clicked the garage-door opener above the visor. As the door slowly creaked up, he turned the key in the ignition, half expecting the battery to be dead, but his extended-cab Ford F-150 pickup came to life without trouble. The engine rumbled as if the truck was saying *welcome home* to him.

"Good to see you too, buddy." Murph drove forward with a smile he meant, the first one in a while.

The boxy white mail truck trudged by just as he reached the end of his driveway. Since Robin Combs was a friend of his, he jumped out to say hi.

"How's my favorite girl?"

She slipped from the truck, spry as anything, her gray hair in her usual bob, angel earrings dangling from her ears. "I thought you might be home. I had a feeling."

He grinned. "I wish you'd have a feeling about the lottery numbers."

"It'd be wrong to try," Robin said in all seriousness, then her face turned even more somber. "You got hurt."

Murph rolled his shoulders. "Nothing serious. How have you been?"

"I'll be moving to Upstate New York to be closer to my sister. I think she's going to need my help with something soon, so I'm retiring."

"What, twenty years early?"

Robin gave a whooping laugh. "If only. Truth is, sitting in the truck for all those years, my back's killing me."

"I'll hate to see you go, and that's the truth," Murph told her. "They might be able to find someone to hand out the mail, but they'll never find anyone half as pretty as you, Robin."

She looked seven shades of pleased. "Pete Kentner's taking over my route."

Murph raised an eyebrow. He knew Pete from high school. He was a couple of years older than Murph, decent guy. "He's moving back home?"

"His mother has cancer, but I don't have a bad feeling about her. I'm pretty sure she'll make it."

"I hope she does."

Mrs. Kentner was a nice old lady, a professional volunteer. Any kind of fundraising, and she was your gal. She'd raised money for everything from the bandstand to a new fire engine. Murph made a mental note to stop in and offer help once he'd gotten a few things squared away.

Robin glanced at her watch. "I should go. Mrs. Torrino will be waiting by her mailbox, if I slip as much as five minutes behind schedule."

She rose to the tips of her toes and pinched Murph's cheek like she used to when he'd been much younger. Murph enfolded her in a bear hug.

"Aw, honey." Her eyes glistened when he let her go.

He waved after her as she progressed down the street, then he drove to the police station, enjoying the ride, looking for signs of change, reassured when he didn't find any. No empty storefronts, not too many FOR SALE signs. He liked seeing his town prospering.

The police department's square brick building, Murph's home away from home, was the same, too, as when he'd last seen it, plain as can be. Nothing fancy inside either: reception, the main area where all their desks stood, the captain's office, the interrogation room and the conference room, then the hallway that led to the holding cells and the evidence room in the back. *Utilitarian* was the word.

"Murph!" Leila, the admin assistant, rushed from behind the counter and gave him a fierce hug. She was a no-nonsense widow with three boys, cropped hair, little makeup, plain clothes, but always the most colorful footwear she could find, her only nod to fashion.

She was wearing red boots with sequins.

Murph gave them an appreciative whistle.

A plate of his favorite chocolate chip cookies sat on the reception desk.

"Bing said you might be coming in." Leila grinned when she saw Murph eyeing the goodies. "Welcome back."

"It's nice to be home." He let her go and went for a

cookie. "Oh yeah." He gave a moan of pleasure after the first bite sent familiar flavors exploding on his tongue. "I remember this. I've missed your baking. A lot." He chewed and swallowed. "How are the boys?"

"Trying their best to drive me to drinking."

"Have they discovered girls yet?"

"Bite your tongue, Murphy Dolan." Leila looked like she might say more, but the phone rang and she ran for the switchboard. "Broslin PD."

"Hey." Harper Finnegan and Chase Merritt hurried from the breakroom to welcome Murph back. "Look who's here."

"Made detective yet?" Murph asked. They were in a contest to see which one of them passed the exam first. Murph had been in the running until his deployment.

"Now he comes back," Harper groused, struggling with a grin. "When all the puke is mopped up and the Deering twins have been sent upstate."

Harper was Broslin's black sheep turned cop, tall and lean, a ladies' man and then some. His parents owned Finnegan's, the best Irish pub in the county.

He flashed a long-suffering look at Chase. "The man treats police work as a holiday."

"If this is vacation, where is the beer?" Murph challenged them.

"You let me know when you find it." Chase gave him a quick, manly embrace, nothing near as demonstrative as Leila's had been.

Chase was the mildest of the bunch, easygoing. Had a reputation for being a big teddy bear, but he could lay down the law and finish a fight with a single right hook if the occasion called for it. Of course, with Chase, that was rarely the case. He was good at talking people down, such an all-around nice guy, even the criminals liked him.

He checked Murph over. "You all right?"

Murph reached for another cookie, smiling his thanks to Leila. "Can't complain. Found a knockout redhead in my bed when I got in last night."

"Shit like that never happens to me," Chase mumbled. "Can I have her?"

"No because she's a human being and a person with body autonomy who makes her own decisions," Murph said. "And talking about women like they're objects is not cool. Welcome to the twenty-first century."

"Did they teach you that in the Army?" Harper put his arm around Chase and blinked his eyes rapidly, as if about to cry. "Look at that, our Murph, all grown up."

Murph flipped them both the bird.

They weren't bad guys, but they did tend to revert to frat bro levels when they met for the first time after a long absence. It came from relief, that they were all still alive, Murph figured. Going overseas was no walk in the park, but being a police officer back at home wasn't a guaranteed retirement either.

"Easy for you to get a date," Chase said. "You have the whole returning-warrior thing going."

"I'd be happy to hook you up with my recruiting officer," Murph offered as he finished his cookie. "Caught the Tractor Trio Gang yet?"

"The FBI is taking the lead." Harper rolled his eyes. "They have a temporary office set up over in Chadds Ford."

Before Murph could ask more about that, the captain appeared in his office door. "I'm sure I said it last night, but it's damn nice to have you back. Come on and let's have a chat."

The change in him was even more obvious under the neon lights than it had been in the dark of night. He looked beat up and beat down, ten years older, as if he was fighting a deadly illness.

Freaking Stacy, dammit. How did something like that happen in Broslin? They had, what? A murder once a year, if that. And it had to be Stacy?

He wasn't going to bring her up, Murph decided as he walked into Bing's office that was dominated by a wide desk and a row of filing cabinets. "Any word from Hunter?"

He'd forgotten to ask the night before. The news about Stacy's murder had thrown him. Hunter was the captain's younger brother over in Afghanistan with the Army.

"Talked to him on the phone last week. He's all right. You ever run into him over there?"

Murph shook his head. "Any news on when he's coming home?"

"Not yet. He wanted to come for the funeral, but it doesn't work like that." Bing sat behind his desk, his eyes haunted. "You ought to take time off and rest. You don't have to return to work right away."

Murph shifted on his feet. "That's what I came to talk to you about." He swallowed the bitterness in his throat as he dropped into the empty chair across the desk from the captain. "I'm not going to pass the physical."

Bing's hand stopped halfway to the stack of paperwork he'd readied. "How bad is that shoulder?"

"Not that bad." Considering that good men had *died* around Murph. "I just need to regain full range of motion and build my strength back up." The shrapnel embedded in the bone hurt like a sonovabitch, but only when he moved the wrong way.

He gave the captain a brief summary, the bare basics: patrol, trap, IED.

Bing watched him with sympathy. "What can I do to help?"

"I'm good. I'm home. I have to straighten out my paperwork with the VA, show up for my physical therapy. I don't think I'm going to need surgery. I want to be back at work as soon as possible."

"You take all the time you need," Bing said. "We'll be here, waiting."

"Thanks."

A moment of awkward silence passed between them as Murph fought the urge to ask about the murder. Then he gave up.

"So, what happened?" He wanted to help. He hated that he hadn't been there when Bing needed him. "Where does the investigation stand?"

The captain's face darkened. "Random crime. She was gardening, went in to wash up, and interrupted a burglary in progress. One bullet through the chest. The ME says she was dead in an instant." Bing's voice broke. He cleared his throat. "Then the bastard ran. Didn't even take anything."

"I could be a pair of fresh eyes. I might see something in the files others missed."

"I appreciate it. But we've been over every detail with a fine-tooth comb. I'll let you know if something new comes up. Your only job right now is to heal." Then Bing added, "You want to take your guns home?" A none too subtle change of subject.

Murph nodded. "Thanks for letting me leave them here."

Before he'd shipped out, he'd brought his personal weapons to store them in his locker at the station. He hadn't wanted to leave guns in an empty house where any teenager might be tempted to break in to host a party. Or where Doug might sell a couple if he was tight on money.

Bing asked a few more questions about Murph's deployment, and Murph answered them, but then he left the captain to his work and walked to his locker.

His two handguns and two rifles weren't exactly an arsenal, he wasn't a collector, but he felt better armed than unarmed. He brought the bag up front to his desk, then took a couple of minutes to run a background check on his unexpected tenant. He had her name and the license plate number that he'd memorized before she left for work.

Her clunker was registered to a William Moser, who was two years dead. Not a red flag all by itself. Moser could be a relative.

Murph ran a search on her name next. Katherine Concord didn't come up in any of the law enforcement databases. She had no prior record.

He opened the state DMV database. The Pennsylvania Department of Motor Vehicles had close to a dozen Katherine Concords. However, the woman living in Murph's house didn't match any of the pictures that popped onto the screen. He checked the photos twice, carefully.

Maybe she was from out of state.

Or maybe she's using a fake identity.

Before he could follow that train of thought, a man about his age strode into the station, drawing Murph's attention from the screen. The visitor moved like a cop, but he wasn't in uniform. He measured up the place like a cop, giving Murph a brief nod when their eyes met, then he walked up to Leila at the counter and talked to her for a minute before Bing strode out of his office to greet him.

Russet hair, jeans and a blue polo shirt that matched his eyes; the guy didn't look familiar from town. Murph raised an eyebrow at Harper. Harper shrugged, then went back to his work.

The stranger's body language seemed guarded. He had a friendly look on his face, but at the same time his expression stayed closed. He talked to Bing for a good fifteen minutes and handed him some papers before they shook hands again.

"Who was that?" Harper called out as the door closed behind the guy, and the captain headed back to his office.

"Jack Sullivan. Moving up here from Maryland. He called the other day, wanted to know if we had any openings on the police force. I told him to bring in his paperwork."

Murph waited. The station and the people of Broslin were the captain's responsibility, and Bing would do what was best for the town, friendship notwithstanding.

"I told him we don't have anything permanent," he said. "I might be able to use him for the next month or two if everything checks out. FBI calls twice a day to send us off on some wild-goose chase with the bank robbery business. I'm falling behind with the regular work." He walked into his office, finishing with, "Whatever happens with this guy, your desk will be here, waiting for you when you're ready."

Murph relaxed. "Thanks, Captain."

The door closed behind Bing, and Murph turned off his computer then shot the breeze with Harper and Chase for a few minutes. They wanted to know about Afghanistan too, and he gave them the synopsis. Then he asked a couple of questions about Stacy that he hadn't been able to ask Bing. But as he headed out, his thoughts mostly circled around Kate Concord, his accidental tenant.

They were going to have a real talk when her shift at the diner ended.

* * *

Mordocai stared up at the ceiling as he sat in a tub of scented water and relaxed. His small rental apartment in Broslin was nothing to brag about, the carpets gross, the curtains fraying, but the old-fashioned cast-iron tub made up for some of that. The water was piping hot, the bath oil lavender. He was an assassin on holiday. He deserved a little pampering.

He did his best thinking in the bath, always had. There was something primordial about being submerged. He would swear he was smarter in water. Even professional assassins were entitled to a few quirks.

He liked this leisure to savor life and his work. He liked that this time, he wouldn't have to rush. Even if his plans had been temporarily upended.

Murphy Dolan had returned unexpectedly. Kate Bridges—Kate Concord now—had spent the night with him in the house. She hadn't popped into her little car and driven to a motel. What did that mean?

Did she know Dolan from her life before? None of the research saved on Mordocai's laptop pointed that way. He was pretty sure this was Kate's first time in Pennsylvania, and, according to that morning's quick search, Dolan had never lived anyplace else.

Could she be one of those women who corresponded with soldiers? They could have become close through email.

Dolan could have offered her his place to stay.

Would the two continue to live together? An extra person in the house would be a complication, although, not an unsurmountable obstacle.

Dolan was a cop and a soldier. He had skills, but they shouldn't be a threat. There were skilled men, and then there were assassins. Dolan and Mordocai were hardly in the same category.

He splashed in the water as he stretched his legs over the side, then he closed his eyes, letting the steam envelop him in a haze of well-being. He had time.

Kate was a job he'd chosen, personal, without deadlines, without restrictions, without a client who would change his mind half a dozen times and try to micromanage. Mordocai could afford to slow dance with Kate Bridges for as long as he wanted.

He'd already become her friend without any difficulty. Yes, she was vigilant, but she was also lonely. He'd chosen the perfect disguise, the perfect persona to sneak past her defenses.

He would see her later in the day and ask her about Dolan then. And she would talk to him because she trusted him.

Mordocai slid deeper into the water. He liked this new game, having the leisure to play. He enjoyed being an assassin on holiday.

CHAPTER SEVEN

"People who write movies about the *slooow* pace of small-town life never worked in a small-town diner," Delia, the other new waitress, said. She was in her early thirties and had a Betty Boop vibe going, which she played up with her hairstyle and clothes.

"For a fact," Kate responded as she passed the woman in the narrow space between two tables, wincing as pain shot up her elbow, her tendons protesting the heavy tray. "High-power executive runs away to the backwoods and waits tables while she finds herself? *Please.* Someone from a corner office with her fancy ergonomic leather chair and AC wouldn't make it here to the end of her first shift."

The busy Main Street Diner, a well-loved fixture of Broslin, served home-style meals and coffee since before the township had been incorporated. Since the town was famous for growing mushrooms, they put mushrooms in nearly everything, including dessert. Eileen, the owner, had a secret recipe for mushroom ice cream, which tasted a little like cream of mushroom soup but sweeter and with allspice. Defying all expectations, it became a favorite of customers, if not the waitresses. A dozen overloaded glass bowls on a tray qualified for weightlifting. Kate hurried on, carefully balancing.

Work was a mad rush, but the diner was more of a home to her than the house she rented, and the people here had become friends even in just a few weeks.

Everyone called each other by their first names; the waitresses knew the regulars and their standing orders. Kate finally memorized enough so she wasn't making too many mistakes.

"We need more portobello quiche on the counter," she said as she sailed back into the kitchen with her new order after dropping off the ice cream for the little league team.

Jimmy, the new cook's assistant, tall and skinny as a pole bean, flashed her a hopeful look as he peeled potatoes in a bucket by the back door. "You got time later? I have a couple of tests coming up next week."

A twenty-year-old drifter with a killer mohawk, he was attending GED classes. He reminded Kate of her sister, Emma, probably because he was almost the same age. He talked about the same bands Emma always raved about, the same kinds of movies. When Kate had walked in on him punching the wall in the pantry, frustrated over a math problem, she'd offered to help him with his studies.

"If you're not busy," he added, looking up at her like a hopeful puppy.

She thought about the talk she was supposed to have with Murphy Dolan after work. They hadn't set an exact time. "I can stay for a short while. If Eileen is still working in the office and we can't get in there, we can walk over to the library."

She picked up three plates of burgers and fries with the special sautéed mushroom sauce—the diner's specialty.

"You da best," Jimmy called after her as she shot through the swinging doors with the tray.

She nearly collided with Delia, so she flashed an apologetic smile. "Sorry."

"You're fine. I saved the last slice of chocolate mousse

pie under the counter." Delia winked at her as she stepped aside.

"You're an angel."

The two of them stuck together, Delia especially eager to make friends. She'd moved to Broslin from Jersey to be closer to her boyfriend. Unlike Kate, Delia planned on staying.

She was hardworking and cheerful. Kate liked her. She was looking forward to sharing the pie and having some coffee with her later, when traffic slowed and gave them a chance to rest their feet.

"Mornin', Kate." Eddie Gannon, the town handyman slash snowplow operator, was sitting at the counter with his giant mug that Eileen was refilling for him. He rented the small apartment above the diner, and because he plowed the diner's parking lot first when it snowed, he received free refills. He waved at Kate.

She sent him a smile. "Hey, Eddie."

Antonio sauntered in and sat in his usual spot in the corner, wearing a flawless Italian suit and designer leather shoes.

He let his gaze travel over Kate. Antonio didn't do anything in a hurry. He even ate as if it was an art form, savoring every meal. The waitresses speculated plenty about the kind of things the man could do with those gourmet lips and slow, lazy hands of his.

"Ciao, bella," he greeted her in a faint Italian accent, repeating it in English in a huskier tone. "Hello, beautiful."

He was a traveling businessman, stopping by the diner every couple of days. He always sat at one of Kate's tables.

"New haircut? You look extra-special beautiful today." The man was a hopeless flirt. He sold high-end European chocolates to specialty stores on the East Coast and brought samples for the waitresses.

Kate couldn't help a smile. "Thanks. The usual?"

"Why the rush? Come sit with me. A man's heart needs the balm of the company of a beautiful woman. Why do we live if we can't have even that?"

"I'm supposed to be working here."

"Couldn't you spare a few minutes for a friend?"

She glanced around. Several customers had left in the past couple of minutes. The ones eating seemed content. Since nobody was waiting for her, Kate pulled out a chair.

The boss wouldn't mind. Eileen liked it when the employees made friends with the customers. She wanted people to feel at home at the diner.

Antonio's chiseled face lit up. He reached down for a package at his feet, then settled it on the table between them. The picture on the box showed a fancy hot chocolate machine. "It's yours. A gift."

Wow. She might have stared googly eyed for a second before she gathered herself.

"I can't take this, Antonio. It's too much. Thank you for thinking of me, though." But, oh God, she wanted it. Saliva gathered in her mouth just thinking about what she could do with a machine like this—double truffle chocolate mocha, for starters.

"We are friends, no?" He tilted his head, his fashionably cut thick black hair framing his handsome face.

"Yes."

"Friends can give friends presents."

"Not this expensive."

"It didn't cost me anything. I have two dozen from the company to hand out as promotional gifts."

Honest to God, her heart beat faster. Still, wouldn't accepting a kitchen appliance imply something? He was handsome. She was lonely. But she wasn't sure if she wanted more between them than the casual friendship they already shared. Making real connections or putting down roots wasn't a good idea. She'd be moving on in a few months.

He flashed a rakish smile. "If you had this, you could invite me over for some hot chocolate."

Over where? She shook her head. "I don't even know where I'll be living tomorrow this time."

"Trouble?" He leaned forward, instantly solicitous, taking her hand.

She pulled it away after a second. "My landlord wants me out of his house."

Antonio offered his help, and they talked for another minute before a young couple walked in, and Kate had to rush off to seat them. She wrote down their order, handed it off in the kitchen and picked up Antonio's pie and cappuccino. She served him, but they didn't have time to talk further. A busload of retirees arrived, coming from the antique shops up on Route 30.

By the time Kate caught her breath again, Antonio had left, the hot chocolate super machine waiting for her, along with a generous tip.

She had to take the box to clear the table. But she was going to have another talk with Antonio about this the next time he stopped by. She didn't want him to think that the gift would buy some kind of personal relationship with her. Maybe, if her tips were good between now and then, she could buy the tempting piece of machinery from him.

As Kate stashed the hot chocolate machine behind the counter, Eileen wiggled her eyebrows. The boss was close to retirement but still had the energy of a woman half her age. Her graying hair, usually in a French braid, would fly behind her as she darted around the diner to serve her customers. She always had a smile on her face, and at the moment, it stretched extra wide. "Things heating up with Antonio?"

"Maybe." Maybe a quick affair with a hot guy wouldn't be a terrible thing.

"He does have a way of looking at a woman, doesn't he? That man is fine enough to sell things on TV that aren't butter." Eileen fanned herself with a laminated menu, but then turned serious. "I didn't mean to eavesdrop, but did you say you were having trouble with your rental? Is everything okay?"

Kate summed up her situation in a couple of sentences,

ending with, "Not a big deal. We'll figure it out."

"I didn't realize you were renting from Murph."

"I didn't either." Which was the problem, obviously.

Eileen dropped the menu back on the stack. "He's one of the good ones. All the way. Antonio is nice, but Murph Dolan is the real deal."

"If you say so."

"When I broke my wrist last spring, he came and dug up my garden for me. Real stand-up guy, unlike his father. His old man used to stagger by here on his way home from the liqueur store. Left shortly after Doug was born."

"Must have been hard on their mother."

"Probably." Eileen shrugged. "I didn't know her well. Died a few years back. From what I heard, she had a mean streak."

Not what Kate had expected. Then again, she knew she tended to over-idealize "normal" families. But just because a kid hadn't been taken by social services, it didn't mean his or her childhood had been a trip to Disney.

Eileen said, "I have my doubts about Doug sometimes, but Murph turned out just fine." She flashed Kate a speculative look. "He's single. He could use a good woman in his life."

Kate knew a matchmaking attempt when she saw one. She glanced around the room. "I'd better see to table three."

She kept on bustling until her shift ended, then she headed straight over to the library with Jimmy.

"Why are you parked at the bank?" Jimmy asked as they walked across the road.

"Delivery trucks were blocking the whole front parking lot when I came in this morning." She never parked in the back lot. Too secluded. She didn't like places where she was isolated or could be easily trapped if Asael caught up with her.

She drove Jimmy over to the library, and they did calculus for an hour, while in the back of her mind Kate worried about Murph.

Jimmy rubbed his eyes. Yawned. "Sorry. Didn't get much sleep. Dude in the apartment next to me moved out last night. Skipped rent. He was dragging furniture down the hallway and down the stairs till four in the morning."

Terrible. But it gave her an idea. "How soon do you think someone else could move in?"

"As long as Tommy didn't put any holes in the walls… Couple of days? Cleaning woman is usually in and out pretty fast."

"What would I need?"

"First and last month's rent, security deposit. Then you're in. As long as you pass the credit check."

Right. That'd be a no then.

Her phone pinged with a text from the mechanic shop. She gave it a quick scan.

"They got the new heater for my car. Have an opening if I can drop it off right now." With the worst of winter still ahead, heat in the car was kind of an important thing.

"Go ahead. I don't think my brain can take any more today."

She dropped Jimmy off at the diner, then moved on to have her Chevy fixed.

Behind Arnie's Gas Station, the gray cement-block shop consisted of three bays and an office in the back. The air smelled like motor oil, the floor had some grime to it, but the locals didn't mind. No frills, no thrills, decent prices.

Her mechanic, Fred Kazincky, waved at her when he spotted her. "Hey, Kate."

He had retired from the job in Upstate New York and decided to head to Florida, but instead of the quick way, he was working his way down little by little, six months here, six months there, taking up temporary employment to finance his East Coast meanderings. He'd spent most of his life in the town where he'd been born. He wanted to try out the life of a nomad, for a change, see some of the country before he showed up for his date with the undertaker. His words.

He wiped his oily hands on his blue work overalls. "Someone had a car inspection scheduled but they cancelled. I thought you might want to jump in."

His movements were stiff from arthritis, his face lined, carrying the mark of a life fully lived. "If you can leave your car now, you could pick it up tomorrow after work. Jackie's coming off shift at the register in a minute. I'm sure she'd give you a ride home." He shuffled toward the office. "Hang on, I'll ask her."

"Thank you. But that's okay. I'd rather walk."

The house she rented waited just a few blocks away, and Paolo's Pizza Palace stood halfway between, selling not only fresh-made pizzas, but all the ingredients needed to make her own pizza at home whichever way she liked. The store even sold pizza stones and offered lessons. She wanted to pick up a couple of things and didn't want to hold up Jackie.

Fred looked unconvinced. "You sure? She's a nice gal. She'd be happy to do it."

"I can use some fresh air. Need the wind to blow the *eau de french fry* out of my hair." And some more time to think. She wasn't looking forward to a clash of wills with Murph.

In fact, making him pizza for dinner might go a long way toward encouraging him to let her keep her lease.

Fred nodded. "I'll look at the brakes too. From the sound they made when you pulled in, they might need some help." He lifted a hand. "Not trying to talk you into something expensive. But you don't want bad brakes."

"Can we keep it on the cheap side?"

"You bet. How are they treating you at the diner?"

"You know Eileen. She's a regular den mother. But I seriously need to get away from those pies." She patted her midriff.

"I could always teach you how to be a grease monkey."

She couldn't help laughing at that. "I'm not sure I have enough years left on earth. I'm not exactly mechanically minded."

"You can do anything you set your mind to, young lady."

He was always this nice; reminded her of her father. Sometimes, when she worked second shift, she brought him pie that Eileen was clearing out of the glass display case at the end of the day. Fred usually picked up extra hours, working at the gas station after the mechanic shop closed. He was around most evenings and loved a late dessert.

He returned the favor by cutting her a break on car expenses, since her clunker needed frequent fixes.

She switched cars often, finding her vehicles from private sellers so as to leave the faintest trail possible. But that meant no recourse and no warranties. Still, it was more important to be safe.

"How is your knee?" she asked Fred.

"Can't say it's better, but at least it's not worse. How are things for you, Kate?"

"Pretty good. Other than possibly getting kicked out of the house I'm renting," she said, then told Fred about Murph's unexpected arrival.

"Want me to have a word with him?"

"I'll let you know, if I can't work it out on my own." It was nice to know that someone had her back. "Thank you. Hey, I could text you some exercises you could do at home for that knee. Would that be all right?"

"I suppose I could try."

"They'll help. You take care now."

Before she left her car, she grabbed the bag that held Antonio's gift. No way was she leaving that—a decision she regretted by the time she'd walked the first block. The small machine weighed a ton and a half. She lugged it on, telling herself she was building muscles.

The three boys loitering across the street from the Pizza Palace, hanging out under the awning of the closed flower shop, checked her out with some exaggerated leers, egging each other on. They were probably in their late teens, twenty at most. The fact that they outnumbered her gave them enough courage for a couple of wolf whistles.

"Hey, wanna hang with us?"

They hassled her again when she came out with her purchases: fresh dough, specialty sauce, handmade mozzarella.

"How come you won't come over? Too stuck up?"

Kate ignored them and hurried on her way, wishing she were wearing pants instead of her short uniform skirt. The wind had picked up while she'd been inside, attacking her in icy gusts. She was ready to get home, and not just because of the weather.

She told herself not to turn back. Then she did, anyway. The boys had pushed away from the brick wall. They were watching her, whispering at each other, laughing.

She picked up the pace, but soon she could hear their shoes on the pavement as they followed. Her stomach clenched as she turned into the short alleyway up ahead. The passage was narrow and dark, but no more than forty feet. Once she cut through, at least she'd be on her own street.

CHAPTER EIGHT

On his way home from the station, Murph stopped by his brother's place.

"About the tenant," he said after they exchanged greetings, sitting out in the garage where Doug had an old couch and a TV set up, along with a kerosene heater. A beat-up fridge in the corner kept the beer flowing. "How did that come about?"

The garage was crowded and dirty, dust-filled cobwebs hanging from the ceiling. Not much to brag about, but at least the place was large enough to hold two cars, plus Doug's little man cave in the back, the only spot in the house where he could almost do whatever he wanted.

He puffed on his cigarette, then hung his head, the overhead light reflecting off the top where his brownish hair had begun to thin. "Needed some extra money to fix the truck. Then this hot chick at Finnegan's said she was looking for a place to crash…" He put on his best repentant face. "I figured, what would it hurt? You're my brother. You'd help out if you could."

"Help you, or her?"

"Both?"

The door that led to the house opened. Everything about Felicia, Doug's wife, was strict and straight-cut, from her hair to her pantsuit. Doug snapped his hand down to hide his cigarette behind his back.

"You need to walk the dog. You could both use the exercise." She let their black Lab out, narrowing her eyes as she sniffed the air. "Are you smoking out here?"

Doug's eyes widened with innocence. He jerked his head toward the heater. "It's just the kerosene."

She shot him a glare that could have set that kerosene on fire, then yanked the door closed without another word.

"She's right. I could use the walk." Doug patted his potbelly with a sheepish look. "I did pile on a few pounds recently."

Bella, the dog, ran to greet Murph, and he scratched behind her ears. "There you are, girl. Look at you. Happy to see me?"

Bella put her front paws on his knees so she could lick his face, the warmest welcome Murph had received in this house yet.

Doug pulled his cigarette back out and drew on it. "Felicia's been in a mood all week. Women." He shrugged, then blew out smoke and looked at Murph. "Do you ever miss Mom?" he asked out of the blue.

"I think about her." There wasn't much to miss, as horrible as that sounded.

"She used to go after you something fierce."

"She did."

Doug had always been the golden boy. He was four years younger, had always been their mother's favorite. Murph looked too much like their deadbeat father. Nothing Murph had ever done had been good enough. Doug had always been the prince, gotten everything their mother had been able to give, including the house when she'd passed.

"She went easier on me," Doug said in a sentimental tone. "I always thought I had it good."

"You did."

Doug shook his head. "I never learned to fend for myself, not like you." He took a swig of his beer. "Felicia's different."

Maybe. But Felicia could be mean in her own way. Doug had married an overbearing wife because he missed his mother, but Murph had a feeling the marriage wasn't working out for his brother exactly as he'd expected.

Doug drew on his cigarette, then dropped his hand, in case Felicia came back. "Hey, maybe now that you're home for good, you'll settle down and get hitched."

"I don't think so. Not the type." Murph hadn't so much as lived with a woman before. He was very comfortable with solitude.

"Kate's pretty."

"She's moving out."

Doug nodded and bent to tip some ashes into the ashtray he kept hidden under the couch—no matter how many times Murph had told him it was a fire hazard—then looked up. "I already spent her rent money. I can't give back any of that."

"Don't worry about it. How about if we grab a couple of beers at Finnegan's later this week?" Felicia didn't like it when Doug had people over. She was likely to give him an earful for Murph stopping in unannounced today.

"Anytime, bro." Doug grinned with relief.

"Anything new in town that I missed?"

"The old sub shop burned down at the strip mall. Everything's going out of business out there anyway. Internet shopping. Have a delivery van in our driveway every damn day." Doug shrugged. "Mallory's finally divorcing our dumb ass cousin. He brought his internet dates home to the house while she was working. At least, there are no kids." He shrugged again. "Nothing's really going on in Broslin. Couple of bank robberies in the county. I think one was within town limits."

"Bing told me."

"Wonder if they get away with it."

"I wouldn't bet against Broslin PD."

"Now that you're home."

"I won't be going back to work right away," Murph said, and when Doug asked, he told his brother about his injuries.

They talked some about that, and more about what was going on at the lumberyard where Doug sometimes worked. Then, when Felicia came out the second time, glaring at Doug to walk the dog already, Murph took leave of his little brother and drove home at last.

Snow began to fall, swirling in the wind but not heavy enough yet to snarl traffic. People in Broslin knew how to drive in worse. Murph cut through town without any trouble, turned down his street. And saw Kate surrounded by dark shadows at the mouth of the alley.

He pulled the truck up, tires screeching, even as Kate dropped the bags she'd been carrying and went for her purse. *The gun*, he thought, and burst from the cab, unarmed, his own weapons locked in the back of the pickup.

No time to grab anything. One of the boys had a knife out already. Murph ran.

"Hey!" He jumped into the melee and risked getting shot as he faced her attackers. "What are you doing?"

They shrank back, but they didn't scatter. The big one glanced at his buddies. He was clearly the leader of the alley cat gang. The kid didn't want to lose face. He looked familiar. *Robbie something.*

Murph knew the boy's father, had picked the man up before for shoving bottles under his shirt at the liquor store and on other stupid offenses on half a dozen occasions.

The kid sneered at him. "Watcha gonna do, grandpa?"

Murph nodded toward the kid's knife. "You need to put that away. Now."

Instead, Robbie charged at him, screaming obscenities.

As Murph managed to grab the kid's arm without letting the little shit nick him, the rest of the dimwits joined in, pulling their own weapons, a couple of nasty-looking blades designed to give them the street cred they craved.

"Stop!" Murph knocked Robbie back into his buddies, using the minimum force required. He was a cop and a soldier; he'd better be able to subdue three snot-nosed kids without lethal violence. He put on his scary face. "Scram!"

But the idiots were still thinking about it.

Then suddenly, Kate screamed like a ninja and rushed forward, around him, with her gun aimed.

Whatever few braincells the kids had working kicked in, and they backed into the alley behind them, cursing, then disappearing at last.

Instinct pushed Murph to pursue, but rounding up delinquents wasn't his job at the moment. He was on a break from his law enforcement duties. Just as well, since he most definitely didn't want to leave Kate behind.

He reached for her gun. "Let's put this down, all right?"

He didn't want her to accidentally squeeze the trigger and hit one of those boys who might still be loitering in the shadows. Not to mention, he didn't need a bullet in the kneecap either.

He eased the weapon from her stiff fingers and flicked on the safety. "You scared them off."

"Yeah." She glanced down at her hands that began to shake. "Not good."

"It's all right now." He tucked the gun into his belt behind his back. "Fight's over. You were steady when it counted."

Amazing how calm he could sound while he wanted to slam his fist into something. Or someone. Or several someones. If they weren't fricking kids.

While she nodded, pale-faced, he pulled his phone, called the station, caught Harper on the other end and told him what happened, which way the kids were heading, what they wore and what information he had on Robbie. Then, after he hung up, he refocused on Kate.

"I could have shot you." She rubbed her palms against

her hip. "I had my finger on the trigger, and you jumped in front of me."

"That was stupid." And, okay, he wasn't stupid, so why had he done it?

Because he had wanted to protect her not only from the kids but from doing something she would regret later. Killing another person wasn't the easiest thing to live with, regardless of the circumstances.

She looked like she could use a hug. He leaned forward, remembered the landlord-tenant nature of their relationship, and pulled back.

He was silently swearing as he bent to grab her bags, then began walking toward his pickup that waited with the motor still running and the driver's side door hanging open. "Come on. Get in."

She did, sliding in on the passenger side. She stared straight ahead, toward the alley as if worried that her attackers might return.

"Where's your car?" He handed her gun back.

She slipped it into her purse. "At the shop."

"What's wrong with it?"

"Heater."

"Why didn't you call me?"

She glanced at him. "You're not my keeper. We barely know each other." She wrapped her arms around herself. "I don't have your number."

"Let's take care of that right now." He waited until she pulled her phone out, then rattled off his number as he stepped on the gas and headed home. "I'm sorry you were scared. They'll be taken care of. I promise."

She didn't start crying or freaking out. Anybody would have, after an attack. Murph had seen men twice her age react worse.

He was still thinking about her oddly calm demeanor when they reached his driveway. He pulled into the garage, since the snow was picking up.

"I'll take those." He carried her bags into the house

and set everything on the counter, a small appliance that looked like an espresso machine, and assorted ingredients from the Pizza Palace.

She hesitated in the middle of the kitchen. "You don't have to put anything away. I'll be making the pizza in a minute. I'm just taking a quick shower first."

She seemed jumpy at last. Delayed reaction.

As she disappeared down the hallway, Murph almost went after her. *To do what?* Offer her a shoulder to cry on? *Stupid.*

As she'd said, he wasn't her keeper. They barely knew each other. They certainly weren't friends. The urge to comfort her was ridiculous.

Since Murph needed to walk off the adrenaline of the earlier confrontation, he went upstairs and ambled through the rooms he hadn't yet finished. He scanned the ripped-up floors, the doors that lay against the walls and the water-stained ceilings. Not the prettiest sight he'd ever seen, but the house had potential. The place would look just fine after some hard work.

The upstairs was as he'd left it. Kate hadn't spread out. Then again, she seemed to have precious little to spread. She had no personal effects anywhere but the master bedroom and bath, Murph thought on his way back down to his living room, stopping when his gaze fell on his duffel bag next to the couch in the corner.

The bag slumped on the floor instead of leaning against the wall as he'd left it that morning. He strode over and looked inside. The book he'd carried to war—*The Odyssey* by Homer—was on top. He was pretty sure he'd put it on the bottom. His muscles tensed. The incident at the alley had brought out his protective instincts, but as he looked around, his mood turned.

Had Kate come back home after he'd left the house? Had she gone through his belongings? Why? Because she still didn't trust him? Or was she looking for money?

He was almost certain that she was a woman on the

run. But from what? An abuser, or the law?

He hesitated only for a second before he strolled back to her bedroom, stopping in the doorway. He could hear water running in the attached bathroom. She was still in the shower.

Murph scanned the room but couldn't see the purse that held her gun. She must have taken it into the bathroom with her. That too meant something.

The shower stopped.

He rapped on the half-open bedroom door.

"Be right out," Kate called in response. "Almost done."

Murph stepped forward.

No pictures of any kind on the dresser or the nightstand. No correspondence, not even a single bill. Maybe Doug had included utilities in the rent. She had a handful of books—mostly romance novels—on top of the fireplace that currently wasn't operational. No jewelry or valuables. The closet door stood open, revealing clothes he'd seen the night before and a banged-up suitcase he'd missed.

He had a right to know who was living under his roof. He reached for the suitcase and opened it. Empty. He searched through the front pocket and pulled out an old parking pass. *Kat Johansen.* Her real name?

He was going to find out before the day was over.

He shoved the suitcase back in its place, then returned to the kitchen, sat at the table and waited for her. If she was an innocent woman in trouble, he wasn't going to kick her out. But if she was a crook, he was going to make sure she was busted and put away for whatever crimes she'd committed.

CHAPTER NINE

Kate felt better by the time she walked out to the kitchen and set her purse on the counter. She was warm at last, wearing black yoga pants and a simple blue cotton shirt. She was going to feed Murph into culinary bliss, talk him into leaving, then treat herself to double mocha chocolate from Antonio's fancy machine. She deserved that, after the day she'd had.

Murph didn't look like his day had been any better than hers. He was watching her with a dark look on his face as he sat at the round oak kitchen table.

She tugged her shirt down. Stopped herself. *No nervous gestures.* She smiled at him. "Thank you for saving me out there. I appreciate the help."

His eyes narrowed. "Why aren't you more shaken?"

"I've been threatened by bodily violence before." She blurted out the truth, then snapped her mouth shut.

"Care to elaborate on that?"

"Not really." Although, for a moment she wondered what he would say if she revealed that she'd not only been threatened before but had been beaten, brutally and repeatedly. She didn't like talking about that part of her life.

She didn't want people to treat her as if she was a victim. She didn't want to be pitied.

She pulled the hot chocolate machine out of the bag. Just looking at all those levers and settings on the picture on the box made her feel better.

"What's that?" he asked as she set the appliance on the counter.

She pushed a yellow-checkered dishcloth out of the way. "A gift from a friend."

"Who is Kat Johansen?"

The question caught her off guard. A second passed before she could present a suitably blank look, one that wouldn't betray how hard her heart was hammering. "What are you talking about?"

He held up a parking pass she thought she'd gotten rid of when she'd left her previous identity behind. Where had he found that?

"Why do you carry a gun wherever you go?" He indicated her purse with his head.

"It's a free country. Second Amendment. I'm a woman living alone." Let him take his pick.

"You have a concealed weapon permit?"

Dammit. How did she end up renting from a cop? She should have asked Doug more questions. She needed to be more careful than this.

She reached for the Pizza Palace bags. "I should start cooking. I'm so hungry I can't see straight. Aren't you starving? How do you like your pizza?" She smiled. "It's going to be all-fresh, homemade."

"How about we go down to the station, run your prints and see what the system kicks out? I wouldn't mind knowing that the person making my dinner is not, say, wanted for murder."

She whipped back around to face him. "I'm not. I promise."

"You're not Katherine Concord either." Murph had an I-mean-business look on his face, hard determination that said he wasn't going to let her wiggle out of this. His next words confirmed her fears. "You're hiding something, and neither of us is leaving this kitchen until I find out what. It's that simple. Let's do this the easy way."

She clenched her jaw. Nothing had been easy since she'd walked into Marcos's penthouse apartment two years ago and watched him bleed to death. The thought that Murph was too observant by far, too smart to fool, scared her.

He folded his fingers together on the table in front of him. "I'll make it even easier. Why don't you just answer a couple of questions?" He started with, "Are you in trouble with the law?"

"This is ridiculous." She moved to unpack the first Pizza Palace bag, turning away from him again. She didn't want him to see her face as she lied. "Of course not."

Except for maybe a few counts of identity theft.

"You hesitated."

Sherlock freaking Holmes. "I don't want the law involved."

She turned the oven to 450 degrees, brand-new, stainless steel like all his other appliances. Most of the house needed work, but the kitchen had been updated, a pretty nice space, or it would have been if Murph Dolan wasn't sitting in the middle of it, scowling at her.

"Are you hiding from someone who is trying to harm you?" he asked. "I can protect you."

Maybe he could, if she trusted him enough to tell him the truth, but she didn't. They'd known each other, what, two seconds? She stepped to the fridge to escape his searching gaze.

"Why did you go through my bag?" he asked from right behind her, making her jump. He'd come around, his socked feet silent on the tiles. And now he was standing between her and the counter that held her purse and gun, dammit.

He was taller, stronger, twice as wide in the shoulders,

crowding her in the small space. She swallowed. "I didn't touch your stuff."

He took another step closer. "Somebody did."

Who? Had somebody been in the house? Could Murph be right? He'd know, wouldn't he? He was a cop.

A chill ran down Kate's spine, desperation bubbling in her stomach. Her gaze darted around the room. Had Asael found her?

She'd been so careful. She always checked whether she was being followed. She'd chosen Broslin randomly. She kept no ties with any of the places where she'd hidden before, no ties at all with her true identity. Not a single person among her friends and family knew that she was alive.

"I have no idea what you're talking about." She shook her head. Murph had to be imagining things. She stepped around him.

He turned after her. "I'll refund whatever money you already paid Doug. I want you to leave as soon as you get your car back."

"I can't." Her stomach clenched. "This isn't fair."

"I'm not going to have someone I don't trust in my house. I'm sorry for whatever troubles you're facing. I can't help you if you won't tell me what's wrong." He paused. "If you're running from someone, I need to know who it is. I have a right to know who might be showing up at my door, looking for you."

"Nobody!"

"Fine. When you go, make sure you're not being followed. Do you know how to do that?"

"Keep track of the car behind me." She'd been doing that forever.

"If whoever you're hiding from is an idiot," he said. "If he has any brains… Keep track of the car two spots behind. Someone following you would drive far enough back so you wouldn't easily see him, but not so far that he'd have to worry about missing you at the first traffic light. Watch out for cars that run red lights behind you."

She blinked at him. He was giving her advice on how to spot a tail. Pretty surreal, considering he was kicking her out.

She glanced toward the window, at the snow that was beginning to fall hard outside. Any harder and they'd be looking at a blizzard. She needed the safety of this house, and she needed her job at the diner until she saved enough to be able to start over somewhere else.

Panic fluttered inside her chest.

Murph kept watching her as he walked back to his seat, giving her room to breathe at last. "I could give Bing a call right now. He probably has something open at one of his apartments."

No, no, no. Bing was the police captain. He'd start with a background check.

Think. What were her options? The middle of winter was a terrible time to be homeless. And, in any case, sleeping in her car was a quick way to have someone call the cops on her. Or have some idiots like the boys in the alley jump her.

She was flat out of choices. Cornered.

"Okay, fine." She hated that she sounded breathless. She filled her lungs. *In control.* She needed to be in control of this, dammit. "I am hiding from someone who wants me dead. I need you to let me stay. I have nowhere else to go."

He gave a thoughtful nod, his gaze not leaving her for a second. "Obsessive ex?"

She shook her head.

He raised an eyebrow.

He *had* jumped to her defense in the alley. Maybe he could help her. God knew, she needed help. If there'd really been someone in the house like he thought… She swallowed hard. "I'm the only witness to a murder."

He stared at her. "Why aren't you in witness protection?"

"I was. He found me."

He sat in silence while he thought about that. Then he

asked. "How long have you been running?"

"A year and a half. You can't tell anyone. I can't take any chances. Please."

He carefully considered her. "Before I promise anything, I want to hear the whole story."

* * *

Murph watched as Kate busied herself with a baking stone and the fresh ball of dough she'd bought. She'd survived on her own for eighteen months on the run, which impressed him. He was starting to like her, and he wasn't sure how smart that was, under the circumstances.

A killer hunted her.

Okay, yeah, he hadn't seen that coming. Her situation was a lot more serious than just a ticked-off ex. Murph wanted details, questions circling in his head as she moved around in his kitchen.

The tight black pants she wore outlined her perfect backside that he would have dearly loved to explore. Whether he wanted it or not, his body kept responding to hers. The soft material of her simple shirt stretched over her chest in a way that he had trouble ignoring. He wished they could have met in a less complicated situation, like at Finnegan's.

He looked away from her, his gaze settling on the rooster-shaped cookie jar he'd received for Christmas from Leila last year. To give Kate time and distract himself, he peeked inside, then pulled out a cookie and bit in. Brown sugar melted on his tongue. "You made these?"

She shot a darting glance his way. "The new neighbor brought them over. Wendy White. Have you met her?"

He nodded. "Seems cheerful."

"And then some." Kate turned back to her work. "I guess she can bake, but she can't cook. She's over at the diner three times a day. For every single meal." She glanced at the time on the microwave. "She's probably there right now. She comes like clockwork, at nine, then one, then five." She slapped the dough around a little, then began stretching it.

Murph shoved the last of the cookie into his mouth then stood up to see what he could do to help, but his phone rang. He glanced at the display and answered the call.

"We picked up Robbie and his crew," Harper said. "They'll be cooling their heels in jail tonight. Thought you'd like to know. Are you coming in to press charges in the morning?"

Murph glanced at Kate. "It's the police. Want to press charges?"

She shook her head.

"No charges this time," Murph told Harper.

A moment of silence passed on the other end, then, "You know what we say about people who don't press charges, right?"

He did. In general, cops preferred to see criminals face the music. "There are extenuating circumstances."

"All right."

Murph thanked Harper and hung up, then went to help Kate with the tomatoes. "You were about to tell me the rest of your story," he prompted. "How about you start at the beginning?"

Kate worked the dough. "I grew up in Northern California," she said with some reluctance, after a minute.

"That explains the slight accent I haven't been able to place."

"I was in and out of foster care for most of my childhood," she said in a matter-of-fact tone, looking at her hands instead of him, as if distancing herself both from him and the story. "I was a pretty prickly kid. Defensive. Didn't trust anyone. I sure as anything didn't like anyone. And I didn't think I needed anyone either. Then I was adopted by the best people on earth when I was twelve. My sister, Emma, too. She was a baby at the time. I love my family with all my heart. I miss them like crazy."

She swallowed. "I am who I am because of my adoptive parents. They saw beyond the hard shell. Before them, my attitude pretty much kept everyone away."

He tried to picture her as a little wildling, and the image came easily enough. "What made you give them a chance?"

"It wasn't any one particular thing." She paused. "It's a long story."

"I have time."

She shrugged. "Okay, so one foster mom had me play poker for money in a dingy basement at a friend's house from time to time. I was good at it. Anyway, after the Bridgeses adopted me, Ellie, my adoptive mom, my *real* mom, found out I liked cards. She learned to play just so we'd spend time together. It was her way of communicating with me. She used to say, 'Life is like a poker game. People get good cards and they get bad ones. Sometimes they get a lot of bad ones, one after the other. When that happens and then suddenly they get a good card, they might think they don't deserve it, and they toss the good card back.'"

Kate shook her head at the memory, a faint smile playing over her lips. "I told her throwing in a good card was stupid. And she told me how coming to their family could be a good card. It could be the winning card, if I had the courage to pick it up."

She paused again. "She talked to me like nobody talked to me before. Like she really cared about me and my sister. She said things I could relate to, made me think. Somehow she gently nudged me onto the right path little by little."

"You were lucky."

"In that, yes. Lately? Not so much."

"How did you get into this current mess?"

"Do I have to tell you?"

"Yes. All of it."

"I met a kid named Marcos Santiago in the system," she said after a moment. "Our lives kept crossing paths. Even after he aged out of foster care, we touched base with each other every once in a while." She drew a deep breath. "Then he was killed. I was there."

Murph shifted closer. "*The* Marcos Santiago?" He'd

been a cop long enough for the name to be familiar to him, even if Santiago had operated on the other side of the country. "You were there the night he was shot?" He shook his head to clear it. "The killer after you is Rauch Asael?"

The revelation stunned Murph more than a little. Asael was as nasty as they got, wanted on three continents. "You should seriously give witness protection another try. I could reach out to the FBI on your behalf."

"Like I said. Tried that, almost got blown up. I don't trust the system." Kate stretched the dough, working with quick, efficient movements, studiously avoiding his gaze.

Murph put the clean tomatoes into a bowl for her as he tried to think back to what he'd heard about the murder. "Rumor had it, Santiago wanted out, and his business partners didn't like it. Why were you with him that night?" Kate didn't strike him as a stone-cold criminal who'd run in those kind of circles. "I don't remember the reports saying anything about a witness."

"The FBI held that back." Her eyes begged for understanding. "I know Marcos wasn't one of the good guys, okay? But he was good to me. We were with the same foster family once. The mother was okay, but when she wasn't home, the father turned mean. He came after me. Marcos put himself between us and fought off the guy. The lowlife claimed Marcos attacked without reason. Social Services believed him. They pulled Marcos and dumped him into a group home. He had it bad there. One of the older kids abused him."

She made a helpless gesture with her hand, even as anger tinted her cheeks red. "The system failed him from the moment he was born, so he decided to work outside the system. I know it wasn't the right thing to do. I told him that all the time. But he wasn't a monster."

Murph narrowed his eyes. "You were close?" *Lovers?*

"Friends." She snapped out the single word, her eyes flashing with impatience. "That night he invited me over for drinks. I spilled something on my dress, went to the bathroom, took too long. When I came out—" She swallowed hard. "He lay crumpled on the carpet. His throat was cut, but he was still alive. He was looking at me. I don't know if he'd called out. He had the music turned up."

She paused for a second, looking fragile for the first time since Murph had met her. Even in the middle of the night with an intruder in her bedroom she hadn't looked like this. She'd held a gun at Murph. But now her eyes filled with uncertainty and grief.

He almost reached out for her. He knew what it felt like to witness the death of a friend, to be helpless to do anything but watch the life drain out of him.

Kate pressed her lips together and gathered herself before he could decide how much physical interaction between them was appropriate. She was good at keeping her act together under duress. He had to give her that.

She rubbed the back of her hand over her eyebrow. "I saw a shadow moving toward the window. I caught a glimpse of the killer's face in the glass. He saw that I saw him. He started to turn." She swallowed. "But then the twins came in the front door, so he just kept moving forward, and he was gone the next second. He'd come down from the roof in the window-cleaning box and cut a hole in the glass. That's what the FBI said."

"And you were the only one to see him?"

"The twins were just inside the door. The wall of the foyer stood between us. They were laughing as they came around. And then they were screaming, rushing back out."

"What twins?"

CHAPTER TEN

Kate rubbed her arm. Marcos had gotten caught up in the whole living-larger-than-life thing. "The twins were his girlfriends."

She didn't think he'd ever taken a woman seriously. She was the only one he'd ever bothered to keep in touch with long-term, the only one who was outside the dangerous life he lived. Marcos never wanted to settle down, never wanted a family of his own. Didn't want to bring a kid into this messed-up world, he used to say.

"And then what happened?" Murph brought her back to the story.

"Nothing good." She had the pizza dough thin enough, so she slapped it onto the baking stone, then brushed it with olive oil to make sure the tomato sauce wouldn't make it soggy. "The killer found me and put a bullet through the windshield of my car while I was driving to work. I was reaching over for my coffee mug at the same split second, or I would be dead. I drove into a tree."

"That's where the scars come from."

She hadn't realized he'd noticed her scars. "Yes." She touched a hand to her throat, then dropped it. "The FBI decided I should fake my death. If my funeral drew Asael, they could catch him." She tossed on the toppings, then smothered everything in soft, fresh mozzarella.

"But they didn't," Murph observed.

She pushed the pizza into the oven. Staying busy kept her going. "Somehow Asael figured out the trap. I took off. If nobody knows where I am, nobody can give me away."

"How long do you plan on hiding?"

"Until they catch him. He's going to run out of luck someday." Basically, she was counting on Asael running out of luck sooner than she did.

Murph rubbed the side of his thumb over his lower lip. "That can't be easy. Always watching, always wondering. It's like that in the Army, but we get to relax when we're on base. There's security there. A soldier can lie down and close his eyes in his barracks and feel safe. It balances out the intensity of being on patrol." His expression turned somber. "You don't get a break."

As she stared at him, she felt the old tightness inside her loosen a little. That he would understand so completely made her feel lighter. "It's like a deathwatch. You know, when relatives gather to wait for someone to die? I feel like I'm always waiting for my own death. I've been to my own funeral, and now I'm doing my own deathwatch. It's all backward."

She swallowed, refusing to let despair take over. She was still alive. And she was going to stay alive. She was going to do whatever it took. "If you could just give me a few weeks, I—"

"You can stay." He shoved his hands into his pockets. "I'm staying with you. You can keep the bedroom. I keep the couch. I'll do my best to keep you safe while you're in Broslin."

A stunned moment passed while she processed his sudden change of heart. Then relief swept through her, sweet relief.

"Thank you," she rushed to say. "You won't even

know I'm here. I promise." And since he looked dubious, she quickly added, "I swear."

She relaxed at last, but the next second she realized what she'd just done, and she tensed again. For the first time ever, she'd told someone her secret. Thing was, if she'd made a mistake trusting Murph, she probably wasn't going to live long enough to regret it. "You can't tell anyone."

"No." He looked toward the window, at the dark night outside, at the falling snow. "Do you think Asael found you again?"

"I don't see how." She glanced at his duffel bag. "Are you sure someone's been in the house?"

"Hell, I'm still jetlagged. My brain's still catching up. I'm not sure of anything." He ran his hand over his face. "Will you be okay here alone for a half an hour?"

"Of course. Where are you going?"

"I need to run out for a second to see about those boys from the alley. You keep that gun of yours close at hand and lock up behind me."

* * *

Murph stood in the middle of the largest holding cell in the back of the police station. Harper was the only one in the office up front; he'd let Murph come back, given him the key.

Robbie and his buddies crowded in the farthest corner of the cell. They didn't look so sure of themselves without their knives, without an escape route, face-to-face with Murph. Under the neon lights, he could see the scruffy crew better than earlier, dirty jeans and wrinkled shirts, frayed sneakers except for Robbie's steel-toe boots. Looked like he'd worked at one point during the day. There was some hope there, at least.

Murph pulled himself to full height but talked in a calm tone, without anger. "This is your last free ride, boys. Look at it as a significant opportunity and take advantage of it."

The two short ones nodded hesitantly. Robbie spit. Murph ignored it.

"Now, Kate, the woman you were dumb enough to harass"—he got to the point he'd come here to make—"is a friend of mine. You so much as walk down the same street as she does, two things are going to happen. One, she's going to shoot your sorry asses. Two, while you're in the hospital, I'm going to come in for a visit. See how we're just talking here?" He paused. "That's not how it's going to happen next time. I'm not going to say a damn thing. This is your first and last warning. Do you understand?"

"Yeah, man," one of the boys he didn't know said with reluctance, while the other one mumbled "Whatever."

Robbie shrugged, hate boiling in his eyes. His pupils were pinpricks. He had his chin down, his hands clenched into fists.

Murph kept an eye on him. "Anybody tell you to go after her? Scare her a little?"

If Asael was in town, he might have set her up to knock her off-balance.

"Just wanted to have some fun," the youngest of the three said gruffly, his nervous glance darting to Robbie, then back to Murph. "Bored, man. No money for nuthin'. We just wanted to scare her and make her run. For, like, a laugh."

Murph watched him for a moment. He didn't think the kid was lying.

Then, out of the blue, Robbie charged with a high-pitched scream, kicking and punching.

Murph deflected the attack. As pissed as he was at the boy, he didn't want to have to beat up a stupid kid. Robbie kicked hard, but as Murph shifted his bulk, the kid ended up kicking the cell's lock with his steel-toe boot. The bars rattled. Robbie grunted in pain, then went for Murph again. Kicked. Missed.

"Last warning."

When Robbie dove forward, Murph simply stepped out of the way. Robbie slammed head-first into the solid steel doorway then staggered back with a stunned look on his face.

"Enough." Murph shook his head at the boys, then he walked out and locked the cell behind him. He had to work to make the key turn. The idiot had kicked hard enough to warp the metal.

"Life doesn't have to be this hard. You don't have to fight everything, every second, all right?"

He dropped the key off at Harper's desk on his way out of the station. "You called the parents?"

Harper nodded. "They said to keep the idiots. I'll give them another hour to contemplate their sins, then call Youth Services. If they agree to do the program at the church…" He shrugged. "I'd just as soon keep them out of juvie."

Murph drove home, thinking about the boys, about Asael, about Kate. Mostly about Kate. She was getting to him. He had to be careful with that, he told himself as he turned down his street and pulled up his driveway.

As he strode into the house, he was immediately enveloped in warmth and the mouthwatering scent of baking pizza. "That smells good."

"Everything okay?" she asked as she put on a pair of yellow oven mitts.

"Couldn't be better."

A pumpkin pie sat on the counter, defrosting. She must have pulled that from the freezer while he'd been gone. Odd how back when he'd left his house for Afghanistan, it hadn't felt like home, but now it suddenly did.

Maybe the deployment made him appreciate all the little niceties. Or maybe the shift had to do with the beautiful disaster standing in the middle of his kitchen in yellow oven mitts, a voice in the back of his head suggested. Since he wasn't comfortable with where that thought led, he shoved it aside and asked some questions instead.

"Are you sure there's no way Asael could track you here? Do you keep in touch with anyone from your past?"

She hesitated as she pulled the pizza from the oven, putting the stone on the top of the stove. "I friended my sister, Emma, a few weeks back on Facebook." She turned off the oven and closed the door. "I made an account pretending to be someone we both knew a million years ago."

"Who?"

"One of the nicer social workers, Teresa. I was ten years old, in and out of the system, by the time Emma was born. Nobody would take me, and I don't blame them. But then Teresa said she'd only place us as a sibling pair, and people suddenly wanted me because I came with a baby."

She pulled off the mitts and put them back into the drawer. "We went to two other homes first. They wanted Emma but wanted to give me back after a few weeks. Teresa insisted that we had to stay together. Then we finally went to the Bridges family, and they didn't just want the baby, they wanted me too."

Murph's jaw tightened. His mother had been no picnic, but he couldn't imagine a childhood like Kate's. "What happened to your birth parents?"

"I never knew the man. I assume he was one of the woman's long list of rotating boyfriends," she said darkly.

He suspected there was more to the story there, but he didn't push. He understood the concept of someone not wanting to talk about their past. "So if someone was watching your sister's social media accounts, they might have somehow figured out that you were connecting with her."

She shook her head. "I was careful. I'm not stupid."

No, she wasn't. "What else? What's the one thing you couldn't give up?"

She chewed her lip.

He waited.

"The life books," she said after a few seconds, and must have seen on his face that he didn't know what those were, so she continued. "I keep online photo books for foster kids. It's just a website. My name isn't even on there. I don't charge any money, so there's no income, no paper trail. Asael couldn't have figured it out."

"Never underestimate the enemy. What do these life books do?"

"Kids don't remember their early years. In functional families, there are stories and picture albums. In dysfunctional families, there's nothing. So you can be a foster kid, say, eight years old, and most of your life you can't remember, and there are no pictures of where you came from, no stories."

She pressed her lips together as if trying to figure out how to best explain. "It's almost as if you didn't exist, a scary and unsettling feeling when there are so many scary and unsettling things going on around you already. You no longer know a single person who's been part of your early life who can tell you about those years. You're with a new set of foster parents, the third or the fourth or the tenth. No roots, no connections. Kids need an anchor to their own lives."

He'd never thought about that but could see now how difficult it might be for a person not to have anything solid to hang on to, not to have what everyone else took for granted: a past. "How do you give them a history?"

"Any foster parent can sign the child up, upload a recent photo, or as many photos as they have from social services. Then I do the thing that cops do when they age kidnap victims to show what they would look like years later, except I do it backward. It's not very hard. I use an app. I post a picture of what the kid would have looked like two years ago, four, as a baby. Put some fun backgrounds on their page, like horses if that's what they like, or fire engines."

She smiled, relaxed for a change, excitement shining in her eyes instead of wariness. This was how she should be, always, Murph thought, doing what she loved, and not running scared.

"I put up a time line with the pictures," she continued, "fancy birthday cakes showing the birthdays, that kind of thing. The kids love looking at their page. It helps them process their life and their losses. They have the account forever. Foster parents can keep up, adding photos and memories." She flashed a wry smile. "Of course, some people think it's just a bunch of nonsense."

"I think it's remarkable." He thought *she* was remarkable. "You had a rough time as a kid."

"I had good people coming into my life, and they made it okay. They made it better." She busied herself setting the table.

He had a feeling she hadn't meant to tell him as much as she had.

"How did you come up with the life books? It's a pretty original idea." He helped by getting out a pair of water glasses.

"I took a business course in college, and the final assignment was to create a business and make a plan for it." She shrugged. "I got a C minus. The professor was concerned over viability, the lack of profit. He was right. Some of the birth parents couldn't care less, and the foster parents receive so little money from the government, it doesn't even cover the basic necessities. So, eventually, I set up the site and made it free."

He brought a roll of paper towels over to the table, watching as Kate gracefully flitted around his kitchen. The attraction had been there since he'd first laid eyes on her. Now it mixed with frank admiration. She gave up being with her family to keep them safe. Okay, most people would sacrifice for family, but she went out of her way for complete strangers, too, spent time helping kids she would never meet.

For the first time, Murph understood why a man might fall hard enough for a woman to give up his freedom. He could understand it, but it still wasn't going to happen to him.

He was going to make sure nothing bad happened to Kate while she lived under his roof, then see her safely on her way.

CHAPTER ELEVEN

The Middle Eastern sun was beating down on the eight-man team so hard, Murph felt like his liver was about to bake. He wiped his forehead more out of habit than need. They didn't sweat, not in this heat. Moisture evaporated as soon as it formed on their skin. Their military T-shirts had white salt rings around the neck and underarms.

His tongue stuck to the roof of his mouth. They'd gone out on morning patrol and had brought four hours' worth of water. Ten hours later, every drop was finished. The routine patrol had turned into a lot more, his team pinned down behind a vineyard's crumbling wall.

Curious lizards darted over the cracked mud bricks. They tilted their small heads, stared for a second or two at the American soldiers surrounded by insurgents, then skittered away.

"How long before reinforcements?" Mick, a tall Texan asked next to Murph.

"Might be hours." The team had taken a couple of bad hits. One man had been killed, and two were wounded. "There's heavier fighting to the south, holding up the reinforcements."

A volley of bullets ripped into the wall, sending dust flying over their heads. The insurgents were getting closer. Soon they'd have cover and the angle to make every shot count. Then Murph's team could be picked off one by one.

Since Murph was the team leader, he had to make the call. Going was as dangerous as staying. He had to pick the lesser of two evils, decide which option was less likely to get them all killed. He considered every angle before he made his decision, knowing they had no guarantees, just two almost equally bad choices. "We're pulling back."

Mick looked at him wide-eyed. "Where?"

"To the wadi." He nodded toward the dry creek bed about four hundred feet from their position. "We'll keep low and find a better spot to make a stand. Maybe we can reach a cave on the other side of the hill." The area was littered with caverns, mostly used by goatherds.

He sent his men first, Mick, Greg, Dave, Tommy, Shorty, Antwan and Rasheem. He stayed back to provide them with cover, ran backward after them and lay down heavy fire to keep the insurgents pinned down and give his team a chance. The first of his men were lurching into the wadi when a disturbed patch of dirt caught Murph's eye, and he realized that they'd been set up, had been purposefully herded that way.

The two IEDs exploded one after the other. Mick was blown to pieces instantly. Greg was nearly cut in half. Antwan lost a leg, Shorty an arm.

Murph felt shrapnel bite into his chest, his shoulder. "Don't move! Nobody move!"

But Dave, half-dead, fell forward.

And the world disintegrated around them when the third IED activated.

* * *

"Murph. Wake up." Kate shook her new landlord's shoulders, then stepped back in case when he woke, he didn't remember where he was or who she was. "Murph!"

His eyes popped open, his entire body tense as if under

attack, his gaze snapping to her.

Moonlight illuminated the room enough so she didn't reach for the lamp on the side table. No need for that harsh glare in his face.

"You're home. It's okay. You had a bad dream."

He let his head fall back onto his pillow and closed his eyes, his voice rusty as he said, "Yeah."

Since he wore nothing on top, she could see his muscles relax degree by slow degree. She knelt next to the sofa, onto the blanket that he'd kicked off. She was glad she'd set aside her skimpy nightgown and slept in her yoga pants and shirt. "Want to talk about it?"

"Hell, no."

"You have nightmares like this a lot?"

"Only when I sleep."

"It might help if you tell someone. I mean with the whole PTSD thing."

He shot her a cold glare. "What do you know about PTSD?"

She held his gaze. "Abused children go through something like that."

"Sorry." His muscles tensed again. "But I don't have it. I lost some friends I shouldn't have lost. I can be pissed about that all I want without people hanging some bullshit diagnosis on me."

"It wasn't your fault."

"I was the team leader."

"You didn't kill them."

"No." He gave a hard, cold laugh. "But I sure as hell didn't protect them either."

"You were hurt too."

"I lived to come home."

She nodded. "I'm glad you did. What happened?"

He stared at her for a long moment, dark storms swirling in his bottomless gaze. "We were pinned down in a vineyard," he began, and little by little, he told her the rest, although she had a feeling he edited out the gory parts. The story still left her horrified and breathless.

He rubbed his bad shoulder as he finished, his muscles shifting, rippling under his tan skin as his powerful body moved. He had a smattering of chest hair that looked natural on him, masculine and attractive. His wide shoulders were impressive, as was his sculpted chest. And the serious six-pack, with a narrow strip of hair starting below his belly button and leading the way to the waistband of his sweatpants wasn't ugly either.

The sudden lust that hit Kate hard and fast threw her for a loop. As she scrambled to regain her mental balance, she blurted out something she'd been thinking about before she'd gone to sleep.

"I'm sorry you don't have a family welcoming you home and rallying around you."

He shook his head. "I talked to Doug."

She could have left him and gone back to bed, but something in his shadowed gaze kept her there. "Are you two close? I told you my less than cheerful family story. You can tell me yours."

His eyes narrowed, a predatory gleam coming into them. "I'd rather play the I-show-you-mine-you-show-me-yours game."

Heat crackled in the air between them. Something inside her responded. She blushed, even as she told herself he only said what he said to regain the upper hand. He was the quintessential alpha male, and she'd just seen him vulnerable. He wouldn't like that.

She drew up an eyebrow and kept her tone light. "Keep dreaming, buddy."

A wry smile twisted his lips. "I'd rather dream about you than the usual."

Since his words flustered her, she pushed on with the family thing. "Any other siblings besides Doug?"

He shook his head.

"I miss my family," she admitted. "Emma will be twenty-one this year. I can't believe I'm going to miss that party. I'm the older sister. I'm supposed to be making a big fuss over her and..." She trailed off, watching his left arm shudder against the white cotton sheet that covered the couch.

He held it down with his other hand. "I've got shrapnel in there. Probably some nerve damage."

"What's your treatment plan?"

"I'll get that once the VA processes my case. They're backed up."

"How much pain are you in?"

"I'm fine."

Right. Now that she thought of it, she couldn't remember seeing him use his left arm.

"Let me see." She tugged the pillow from behind him. "Lie flat on your stomach."

His eyes narrowed, but after a moment of hesitation, he flipped over.

Heat radiated off his body as she placed her hands on him. She started gently, feeling her way around, warming up his muscles, looking for the hard knots and tangles. She was especially careful; she didn't want to move or dislodge the shrapnel. But if she could relax his muscles, his entire back and neck wouldn't be a tightly wound, painful mess. She started with his trapezius then moved on to the deltoids.

He was stiff all over, long minutes passing before he began to relax and gave himself over to her kneading fingers.

"Where did you learn how to do this?" The couch cushion muffled his voice.

"I used to be a massage therapist for traumatized children. There are kids who've never been touched in a way that didn't hurt. We tried to rehabilitate them so they'd be able to accept affection and physical contact. Turns out humans really need that to be healthy individuals."

"Is this what you did for a living? Before you had to go on the run?"

"Yes. First the kids get talk therapy. Then, when

they're ready, they might get sent to us as part of their physical therapy needs."

"Children who were hit or sexually abused?"

"Yes."

He waited longer before asking the next question. "Is that what happened to you?"

She should have been prepared for the question, yet it caught her off guard. She'd been too focused on Murph. Her hands stopped on his back. She normally avoided all discussion of her pre-adoption life.

"Sorry," he said. "I have no businesses asking."

She drew a cleansing breath. "She didn't let it happen. I owe her for that. She used to get jealous if her boyfriends so much as looked at me. When I was nine, one of them caught me alone and pushed me up against the dresser. She walked in, before anything bad could have happened. She was furious at me. She told me I better not spread my legs for a man. It'd burn like hell, he'd tear me apart and leave me with a bastard. I suppose that was her birds-and-bees talk."

Her fingers clenched. "I didn't want to burn. I knew what that meant. She pressed her hot curling iron between my thighs as punishment the week before for stealing bread from the cupboard."

"Jesus."

The hoarseness of Murph's voice snapped Kate out of whatever rare sharing mode she'd slipped into. She went back to the business at hand. She flexed her fingers and began untangling his trapezius. "Let me know if anything I do hurts."

But all he said was, "Please don't stop," in a voice filled with gratitude.

She worked over his entire back, down to the lower back, then up again and down the arms, up to the neck. When his muscles were all warmed up and fully relaxed, she returned to the trouble spots.

She visualized the aching knots under his skin, then she

visualized them dissolving. "Try to think of something relaxing and happy."

She always thought healing thoughts as she worked. She believed in bringing positive, healing energy to what she did. She'd had plenty of practice, so it came without trouble, a calm enveloping her as she kneaded his muscles. She'd missed that calm. She'd been on the run for too long, fear becoming her norm.

For this moment, at least she wasn't alone. Focusing on Murph helped her forget her own troubles a little. Then, as minutes ticked by, her fingers gliding along his skin, over hills and valleys of muscles, something strange happened.

Her fingertips tingled. His heat spread up her arm and spread through her. *So completely unprofessional.* She squeezed her eyes shut. She was better than this. He might not be her patient officially, but she was doing this to help him.

She lightened the pressure to wind down the massage, and cleared her throat. "That should help a little. Does your back feel better?"

He stayed facedown for another second or two, then turned his head to look at her. The heat in his gaze stole her breath.

"Thank you." His voice, raspy with desire, skittered along her skin. "Much better."

She sat back on her heels and folded her fingers in her lap so she wouldn't reach out to touch him again. She was fairly sure he would respond. Then they would… Even as need zapped through her, she knew what a terrible idea that would be. The smartest thing was to walk away.

Except, before she could rise, he sat up, legs apart, and she suddenly found herself kneeling between his powerful thighs, his heated gaze holding hers. He shifted forward while reaching for her at the same time, his large hands warm on her arms, tilting her closer to him. She had zero will to resist. Every cell in her body begged for him.

He held her a hairsbreadth from his lips. Then his eyes darkened, and he closed that minuscule distance, their lips meeting at last in the lightest of touches. An electric charge shot through her, short-circuiting her brain.

She wanted more, with a deep, aching need. She could have cried when he pulled back an inch.

"Here is the truth, Kate." His voice turned hoarse. "I want you."

The air disappeared from her lungs. She couldn't speak.

After a tension-filled moment that lasted an eternity, he let his hands drop from her arms, pulling back all the way. "But I'm not going to take advantage of you. You should go back to your room."

She already missed the warmth of his touch, of his lips, as she pushed to her feet, almost as relieved as she was disappointed. Seconds passed before she found her voice. "Goodnight, Murph."

He was right. They needed to keep cool heads. They were strangers, and she didn't like feeling this out of control. She was in no position to lose her head, lose her focus. She couldn't afford to be distracted. Too much was at stake.

She walked away.

When she glanced back from the bedroom door, she found that he'd lain back down, on his good side, facing her.

"Good night, Kate."

The look of open need on his face said he was thinking about coming after her. He didn't. Which was good, because she would have been lost if he did.

CHAPTER TWELVE

Murph woke on the couch from a dream where he was with Kate, playing naked wrestling.

Sadly, in real life, she was quietly making coffee, ready for work in white top and short tan skirt, her plain white sneakers already on her feet.

He liked the dream better.

Those endless legs were going to do him in. His fingertips itched to stroke the length of them, to caress the soft spot behind her knees. His fingers would pave the way for his lips… Murph looked away from temptation, up at the ceiling.

"Hey," she said softly. "How do you feel this morning?"

"Fine." He barked the single word, mad at himself for touching her in the middle of the night, for having dreamt of her, then continuing that fantasy when he'd come awake. She deserved better than him gawking at her and being dragged into his dirty fantasies.

"Any more bad dreams?"

Jesus. He didn't need to be checked up on. He didn't need a nursemaid in the night either. He had nothing wrong with him a hard workout wouldn't cure. He needed to hit the gym at the police station until he was fit enough to pass his physical. Once he got his old life back, everything was going to be fine.

He rolled off the couch and strode down the hall to the bathroom. By the time he came out, his eggs and bacon were waiting for him, along with coffee.

She smiled at him—a sincere, open smile.

He breathed in the heavenly scents, embarrassed for his surly attitude. His problems weren't her fault. "Thank you for breakfast."

"You're welcome."

"I'm sorry I woke you up last night."

She paused by him on her way to the fridge. "I'm not. If the massage helped, I'd be happy to do it again."

The need for her touch washed over him in an overwhelming wave. He looked into her sparkling-sky gaze, got lost a little. A long moment passed before he tore himself away, clearing his throat.

"I'll run into the station after I drop you off at work, then see what needs to be done around the house," he said, so he wouldn't say *I want you*, again.

What the hell was wrong with him? He went to sit at the table.

She tilted her head. "You're injured. Give yourself time to heal. Maybe go for a walk. It's supposed to be a beautiful winter day."

Who the hell had this kind of positive energy in the morning?

He decided to test her. He nodded toward her coffee cup. "Is the cup half empty or half full?"

"It's all the way full. Half of it is coffee, the other half is air. Technically."

He shook his head. "It's worse than I thought."

She smiled. "My mom taught me that. When I came to her, I was just as likely to hurl the cup across the kitchen in a fit. She's a big believer in positive thinking."

"Ellie Bridges?" Her adoptive mother.

She nodded with a wistful expression. She missed her family, but she was soldiering on, doing what she had to do to keep them safe.

Of course, he was attracted to her. Who wouldn't be? She was smart, beautiful, and compassionate. He wanted her, fine. But he was in no position to enter that kind of complication at the moment. And, truthfully, neither was she.

He rolled his shoulders. The pain didn't seem to be as bad as the night before. "How did you get into massage therapy?"

"I wanted to be a veterinarian when I was younger. I think just about every preteen girl does. It comes right after the princess phase."

He nodded, although, he had no idea what she was talking about. "I wanted to be a superhero, a police officer, and a soldier."

She flashed a quick smile. "You got two out of three."

"What happened with the vet phase?"

"My mom set up a volunteering gig at a nearby farm for me where they were rehabilitating abused animals. One of the women there did these therapeutic rubdowns on traumatized horses. She was amazing. She'd start with a horse that wouldn't even allow a human in the corral with him, and by the time she was done, she had a healthy animal that would let people on his back again."

Every time she talked about helping others, she had a sparkle in her eyes, Murph thought as he ate.

She tucked an escaped lock of hair behind her ear. "By the time I went to college, I knew I wanted to work with abused children. At one point, it occurred to me that there might be something like therapeutic massage for people with psychological damage. Turned out there was, and I never looked back."

"You miss that kind of work." He wasn't asking. He could see the truth on her face.

She pressed her very kissable lips together. "I'm going to get back to it someday."

"I hope you will."

He finished off his bacon and eggs, plodded off to a quick shower, then drove Kate to work.

She smiled at him as he navigated traffic. "You're not a morning person, are you?"

"What gave it away?"

"Oh, I don't know. It's just a feeling," she said with barely disguised mirth.

Her dancing eyes almost made him laugh. And he didn't laugh in the morning as a rule, dammit.

He dropped her off then drove to the police station. Everybody was out on calls, Leila busy at the switchboard.

"Morning, Murph."

He responded with a "Morning, boss," and a wink. "Everybody knows you run the place."

She flashed him a *damn-right* grin.

Murph left the weights alone since he didn't want to mess with the shrapnel, but he spent an hour on the treadmill at the station's small gym. He had to build back his stamina if he ever hoped to pass that physical.

After his workout, he went up front and logged into his computer. He didn't have full access to the FBI's database, but a lot of that data was fed into the general law enforcement systems. He used those to learn a little more about Rauch Asael.

The hit man was a serious psycho. The bloody crime scene photos Murph paged through on his computer turned his stomach and brought back memories of gunfire and explosions, his friends dying around him.

Rauch meant smoke in German, he found out. Probably because the man was as elusive as smoke.

Asael was one of the names used for the devil.

And that was just one of the hit man's dozen creepy aliases.

* * *

The small apartment grew cold in the mornings. The windows let wind whistle through, the hideous country curtains not nearly enough to stop the draft. Mordocai could afford better. Or he could have demanded that the super fix things, but he didn't. The character he played wouldn't. He wore the apartment like a costume on stage, like he wore the character's clothes, the makeup, the voice he created for this particular time and place.

He sat by his small desk, holding a new disposable cell phone as he listened to the man on the other end, one of a handful of people who knew how to reach him. A listing put on a certain popular online auction site with the right keywords, and Mordocai would call.

"It needs to be done very quietly and very fast," the man said.

"How fast?"

"By the end of the week. The idiot cannot be allowed to talk at the press conference that's scheduled for Monday. It's imperative for the client. He's willing to pay the rush fee."

"Do you have all the information I need?"

"I'm posting it right now. It'll self-delete in ten minutes. He's in Canada."

They used an obscure Internet chat room, with name, address, license plate, anything and everything they had on the target, posted in code. Most likely, nobody would stumble on it during the short time before it disappeared. But if anyone came across the posting by chance, they would take the few lines of jumbled text for a computer error.

Mordocai hesitated for a second. He'd had his fun stalking and catching up to the witness bitch. He'd talked to Kate. He'd reached out and touched her. He'd been inside her house. Now that he had her in the crosshairs, the thrill was waning. He needed to finish and move on.

He leaned forward in his chair. "Tell the client to consider the job done. Any specific instructions?"

"It has to look like an accident."

By far, the most common request.

Mordocai hung up, went to the chat room and picked up the contract information, then reserved a one-way ticket to Montreal for Friday night. That would leave him three days to deal with Kate.

He'd been waiting for either her or Murph Dolan to move out. He didn't have exact plans for how to end her, but he knew he wanted to play with her a little first, which would be best done in private. He frowned at the thought that he might not get that.

He would just have to be creative.

Method of death?

He hadn't been able to decide yet, but now that he had a time limit, it helped him focus. The perfect ending popped into his mind.

Decapitation.

No one asked for that anymore, but he liked the medieval mood of it. Made him feel like a warrior.

He sprawled in his chair with satisfaction.

In three days' time, he would have Kate Bridges's head on a platter. Then he'd go and take a suite at the Montreal Ritz-Carlton. He glanced around the cramped room. He was done with this dump and the boring little town of Broslin.

CHAPTER THIRTEEN

Since Fred had her car, Kate had to walk to the mechanic shop after her shift. She didn't mind, even if the weather was a little nippy.

"Hey, Kate." One of her regular customers passed her, a retired schoolteacher.

"Hi, Verna. Nice coat."

"A gift from my sister."

Verna stepped into the Irish bakery, and Kate kept walking.

She tried not to think of Murph or the almost kiss. They'd both been half-asleep. Nothing happened. And *nothing* would continue to happen.

First step was to stop her lips from tingling every time she thought of him. Maybe if she didn't keep reliving the moment… She forced her attention to her surroundings.

She liked the town, more so than any other place where she'd hidden so far. Main Street was all red, white and green, the Christmas decorations still up everywhere, even on the gazebo/bandstand in the middle of Broslin Square. The bandstand was usually decorated in red, white and blue, but some elf had added evergreen garlands to the railing for the holidays.

"Hello, Kate."

"Hi, Mrs. Miller."

Then an Amish buggy passed by, horseshoes clopping on the pavement, the sound making Kate smile. The horse parking spots at the grocery store still tickled her funny bone every time she saw them.

Out at the edge of town toward Lancaster, Amish farms dotted the landscape, but Broslin had plenty of modernized farms too, and a lot of places that raised horses. Pennsylvania horse country, the locals called it and told her to wait till she saw the foals in the spring.

Except, she'd be gone by then, disappearing in the night with nothing but a note to Eileen about a family emergency. A day or so later, she'd call to make sure Eileen wasn't worried enough to call the police. She'd tell the boss she wasn't coming back. She'd make up a story, lie through her teeth to people who had given her nothing but kindness. No forwarding address would be offered.

She had to keep moving to stay safe. She couldn't afford to grow complacent. Kate pulled her coat closed against the wind, her fingers hesitating on the top button when a dark blue sedan caught her eyes because it was going at a snail's pace, snarling traffic.

Following her?

She hurried past the Italian butcher, then turned down the next street. She kept an eye on the cars on the road, but didn't see the dark sedan again.

By the time she walked into the mechanic shop, Fred was waiting for her, wiping grease off his hands. "Just finished. Good as new." He patted the hood of her ancient green Chevy with affection.

A few scratches etched the doors, two shallow dings decorated the hood, but the clunker was hers and paid for. The car got her where she needed to go and was cheap enough so regret wouldn't kill her if she had to abandon it in a hurry.

She offered Fred a sincere smile of gratitude. "Not freezing on my way to work will be nice. Thank you so much. How much do I owe you?"

"A hundred-and-sixty-eight bucks."

She counted out the bills from her tip roll. She worked strictly on a cash basis. A bank account and bank card could be tracked too easily.

"You kicked that pesky landlord out yet?" he asked as he accepted the money.

She shrugged. "He might be slightly less annoying than I first thought. How's the knee?"

Fred folded the bills into his pocket. "Better. I've been doing the exercises you sent. When the young whippersnappers aren't watching." He glanced toward the younger mechanics in the back of the shop who were checking her out. "I get enough old-man jokes as it is."

"Don't listen to them. You're the best of the bunch, and everybody knows it."

Fred's wrinkled face stretched into a proud grin. "At least I can still tell what's wrong under the hood, without a dang computer."

"Exactly."

Kate thanked him again, then drove home, enjoying the small-town sweetness around her, that, every once in a while, someone she knew would wave at her. She was going to miss Broslin when the time came to leave.

She slowed as she neared Murph's place, then pushed harder on the brake when she spotted a dark blue sedan by the curb a few houses up. As she watched, the car pulled into traffic, the driver nothing but a black shape behind the steering wheel. Kate could swear it was the same car she'd seen earlier.

She backed into the driveway, facing out toward the street. Better have her car ready, in case she had to make a speedy escape.

* * *

Murph stood at the stove, watching her come in. She

looked beautiful even after a long shift of running around at the diner. "I'm cooking tonight. You take a break."

He'd gone to the store, although he didn't have to buy much. Kate kept the fridge and kitchen cabinets well stocked. He wondered if having a lot of food around made her feel safe, if it all went back to being hungry as a kid.

Since the thought of her being beaten up and starved filled Murph with cold rage, he focused on the stove. "I'll take care of everything. You relax."

"How very modern of you." A quick smile lit up her face. "What's for dinner?"

Her sparkling-sky eyes knocked him off-balance once again. "Steak and potatoes."

She glanced at the counter. "And beer?"

"It's practically a vegetable."

She rolled her eyes and mumbled something about men.

"It's made from a plant." There, let her try to argue with that.

"How about I toss together a salad?"

"Ever heard of vegetable overdose?"

"Not really."

"It's underreported."

She shook her head, but she was still smiling. And she came into the kitchen to make that salad.

He'd been looking forward to her coming home, he realized. For the past couple of months, all he'd wanted was to be back in his house and alone at last. But now that he was here, he didn't mind company as much as he'd thought he would.

She grabbed a lettuce from the fridge and went to wash it in the sink. "The other day," she looked at him, "when you said you thought there was someone in the house. Do you really think someone could have snuck in?"

"I thought things inside my bag weren't as I left them. But like I said, lag."

She hesitated. "Today, on my way home, I thought a

car was following me. Going slower than traffic, acting weird." An annoyed frown flashed across her face. "Then again, it could have been some distracted teen, texting. The longer I'm on the run, the more I start thinking that everyone is out to get me. I wish the FBI would catch Asael already. This is driving me crazy."

Murph turned the steak, premonitions circling in his mind. "I saw a dark, four-door sedan parked a couple of houses down the road the night I got home. One person behind the wheel. He just sat there, then took off."

"It could have been anyone."

"Maybe." He filled his lungs. *Shit.* "The smartest thing to do is operate under the assumption that Asael is here."

She stared at him for a moment, then set the salad into the glass bowl on the counter and wiped her hands, a stricken expression erasing all her earlier lightheartedness. "I have to go."

By the time he asked, "Where?" she was halfway down the hallway.

He turned off the broiler and went after her, found her tossing clothes into her suitcase. "You're taking off?"

He didn't want her to go. A stupid thought. He'd come home to find peace and quiet. Doug had let her into the house, without permission. She had no business still being here. If she left now, Murph's life could return to normal, everything going back to the way it was before his deployment, just as he wanted.

Or did he?

He swore under his breath. Leave it to a woman to completely mess up a man's head. Of course, she had to go. He wanted her safe. "I can call the FBI for you while you pack."

She barely spared him a glance. "No."

"You can't keep running all alone. You need help."

She shook her head. "You don't know how much I want this nightmare to be over, to be able to go home. That's all I want. But moving is surviving. Keeping in motion has kept me alive for the past eighteen months."

"It has." He shoved his hands into his pockets. "And before too. When things were really bad at home, a social worker came, moved you somewhere else where you were safe for a while."

She blinked. "Until they gave me back."

He kept control of the dark rage that rose inside him at the broken look in her eyes. "Until they gave you back."

She sank onto the bed behind her, onto the pretty patchwork quilt that was too small for his sprawling mattress. She closed her eyes and buried her face in her slim hands. A long moment passed before she looked up.

"I associate safety with moving around with my family. My father, my real father, not the biological, was the person who set up new locations for his company in various states. I loved when we moved, because I thought the woman who gave birth to me wouldn't be able to find me."

A small, sad smile played around her lips. "Ellie told me I was legally adopted, that the birth mother's parental rights were terminated and she could never get me again, but I didn't believe it. So every time we moved, I felt safer. I figured if the woman couldn't find me, she couldn't take me back."

Murph nodded. "Running is your go-to coping mechanism, and it served you well until now. That's difficult to abandon. But the FBI could set you up in a safehouse. You could stay in one place for a while. Maybe a long while. Build a new life."

Kate considered his words. "Would you trust them with your life? If they already failed you once."

He hesitated. "Probably."

"Probably not."

"It's different with me."

"Because you're a big, strong, macho man?"

"That too. But also because I have police training. And Army training. I wouldn't run. But we're not talking about me."

She measured him up. "What would you do?"

"Can't imagine running for the rest of my life," he said honestly.

"Running implies you're alive."

"I'd rather not be out in the open, going into unfamiliar territory. I wouldn't want to lose home-court advantage and make myself an easier target. I'd take my chances and make a stand here."

"Against a professional assassin?"

"He's just a man. And, like I said, I have training. I'd set up a trap."

"And you think it would work."

"I'd make sure it did."

She rubbed the palms of her hands over her hip bones, blinking as she considered his words. "Could it work for me?"

"No. Your best bet is the FBI."

"Like you said, he's just a man. If I could set up a trap..."

"You need to be in a safehouse. You tried a trap before. Fake funeral ring a bell?"

"That was the FBI's trap. And it did fail. And that's why I don't want to involve them again."

He couldn't argue with that.

"But if there was another way." Hope sparked in her eyes. "If I *could* set up a trap that worked... Then it's over. Then I'm free forever."

"You're not an action heroine from a movie."

"But I'd be fighting for my life. That's a lot of motivation." She held his gaze. "How would I go about making a plan?"

He remained silent.

So she added, "Hypothetically."

"You start by looking at the situation with as much impartiality as you can and chart a course of action that will lead to the most desirable outcome." He thought about it for a second. "We could be under surveillance right now.

Targets." He moved forward to kneel in front of her on the ancient braided rug by the bed, the way she'd knelt in front of him to take away the pain from his back in the middle of the night. He reached for her hands, her slim fingers disappearing as he folded his around them.

She didn't pull away. "Let's say, I stayed. I am a target. You're not. Are you sure you can't live with your brother for a while? You don't need to be involved in any of this."

"If you stay, then I choose to be involved, dammit." Did she think he was going to stand aside and hide while she was hunted?

Silence stretched between them.

"Maybe I'm just being paranoid," she said after a few seconds. "Maybe he's not even here. I mean, if he's around, why hasn't he tried to come and get me yet?"

Murph thought about it. "Maybe he's still getting the lay of the land. Then I showed up. You're no longer alone in the house at night." He shook his head. "You need to call the authorities in on this."

"You're just saying that because you're a police officer. That's probably your answer to everything. In the hypothetical situation of you setting a trap, would you call in the police?"

"Probably not." He didn't want to lie to her. "Just the bastard and me. Mano a mano." Maybe that sounded like stupid macho stuff, but she'd asked for honesty. Truth was, he wouldn't want any of his friends to get hurt.

"I don't trust the police. I don't trust the FBI. They couldn't protect Marcos, and they couldn't protect me before."

"Anybody you do trust?" he asked, exasperated.

"You."

He stared at her. She trusted him—with her life. That was a lot. Maybe too much.

Then she threw him even more off balance by saying, "I have a gun. You can teach me how to set a trap. Then you leave."

"Still trying to get the house for yourself?" he joked, because, hell, what else was he supposed to say? She was completely out of her mind.

"Will you help me?" she asked.

"Absolutely not. You need to go into witness protection. Setting a trap for Asael yourself is a terrible idea."

"It's what you would do. I'd like to be free of Asael forever. I want my life back."

Her quietly spoken words affected him more than if she'd shouted. "Let the FBI set a trap," he repeated.

Desperation filled her gaze. "Because the first time worked so well? You're right. I can't run forever. If Asael caught up with me here, he'll catch up with me again. He'll get me when I'm not expecting it." She pressed her lips together.

Murph got lost in her eyes. He wanted to do whatever he could to keep her safe. Even if he was pretty sure he was jumping straight into insanity. "Fine. We'll set a trap for him *together*."

If she was going to face down Asael, he wanted to be right there. He would find a way to get the bastard before the man got to Kate. He wanted her permanently free of danger. "I'll help."

A tentative smile stretched her lips. She swayed toward him. He leaned forward, and suddenly their lips met. He let them rest against each other. Then he moved, just barely, taking the slightest taste of her, because he thought he might die if he didn't.

She tasted like chocolate.

He'd never found sweets to be a particular turn-on, but here he was, his body instantly hardening. He nibbled some more, claimed more of her mouth. *Sweet heaven.*

His hands went to her waist, then moved up until his thumbs rested under her breasts, twitching with need. He kissed her over and over again, but he didn't push for more, specifically because he wanted to, so damn desperately. He stayed there, touching, wanting, resisting, for as long as he could stand it, before he pulled back.

Her face was flushed, a dazed look of pleasure in her blue eyes. He wanted her more than he'd ever wanted a woman. But he wasn't going to act on the lust that filled him to the brim. Not yet, not until she was safe. Until then, he had to channel his burning need for her into protecting her, so he focused on that.

He cleared his throat. "Asael will want to take you when you're alone. It's the easiest setup, has the least chance for making a mistake or accidentally leaving a witness." A plan slowly formed in his head. "So we make sure you're never alone. Except when we're ready to spring our trap."

CHAPTER FOURTEEN

The sounds of the diner, nothing but a faint background noise, barely reached the back office that was a jumble of filing cabinets with a desk in the middle, the wall covered with horse show posters. Jimmy pushed his bag of hard candy across the desk toward Kate. His hands looked older than they should have for his age, a collection of cuts marring his skin, a burn mark on the back of one knuckle, reflecting the work he did. "Want some?"

She popped a piece of chocolate candy into her mouth. "Thanks. So the two sides of the equation must always stay equal. Whatever you do to one side, you have to do to the other."

Murph was coming to pick her up later, keeping with their plan of her never being alone until they were ready. He also had some pretty extreme ideas about setting up the entire house as a trap.

Kate focused on the here and now before she could freak herself out. Trapping Asael might have been the best way to ensure her long-term survival, but that didn't mean the prospect of coming face-to-face with the man didn't scare the spit out of her.

She drew some circles on the worksheet in front of Jimmy. "See how these two variables relate to each other?"

"It's easier now that you explained it. Kind of makes sense."

They went through a few more problems before finishing for the day.

She glanced at the time on her cell phone. "My ride should be here in a few minutes."

"Your car's broke again?"

"It's a clunker."

Jimmy crammed his papers into a scuffed-up folder. "So the dude that dropped you off this morning is like your new boyfriend?"

"Just a friend."

"He was definitely checking you out when you were walking away from his truck."

Was he? She bit back a smile. Her love life hadn't been much to brag about before she'd gone on the run, and had been nonexistent since. She couldn't afford to let anyone in. Murph was the first and only person who knew the truth about her.

In a world where she couldn't trust anyone, finally having someone on her side felt both scary and nice, brought a sense of closeness. The two of them living in the same house, sharing the same bathroom, sharing meals, created a sense of intimacy as well, made her feel like they had known each other for much longer than they actually had.

Then there were those charged moments between them when Murph touched her and looked at her with such fierce hunger it made Kate's head spin. *Sweet chocolate-covered cherries.* The man could be intense.

"What are we studying tomorrow?" she asked Jimmy.

He groaned. "Western Civ. Eileen will be doing payroll, so we can't use the office. Want to come over to my place?"

* * *

Murph parked by the curb in front of the diner and scanned Main Street. He checked every car, every person who walked by, but didn't see anyone acting suspiciously. Or many strangers. He knew most of the people.

The mail truck stood in front of the bank across the road, and when Robin walked from the building with half a dozen empty plastic mail trays, Murph beeped the horn.

She looked at him, waved and hurried across when the light turned red and the cars stopped coming. "I was hoping I'd run into you today. I had a dream about you last night."

He winked at her. "Were we naked?"

She laughed, her signature angel earrings dangling as her head moved. With her trim figure and stylish bob, nobody would have guessed that she was nearing retirement. "Men. You do have a one-track mind."

"It's so much simpler that way."

Instead of laughing again, her face clouded. "You were in the woods. You had handcuffs on, and you were shooting at a water tower. It was a dark dream."

"Okay," he said carefully. He'd forgotten over the last eight months how strange Robin could be. She'd been born in Lily Dale, a psychic community in Upstate New York, and proud of her heritage. She handed out warnings and visions as enthusiastically as she handed out the daily mail.

"Just be careful, that's all." She gave his arm a motherly pat. Then the concern disappeared from her face the next second, and she brightened. "And there was a love dove." She smiled. "I caught a glimpse of a wedding at Broslin Chapel."

"Ah." He coughed, choking on his own spit.

Robin flashed another smile, then hurried back to her truck. Murph stared after her, about to ask what the hell all that meant, when Kate stepped out of the diner and distracted him. His brain zoomed in on her, the background fading away.

She had to be tired after running around for the past eight hours, but she didn't show it. As always, she had a smile on her face. He liked the way she walked, the sass in her stride, although he didn't think she was even aware of the positive energy she carried with her wherever she went. He watched as she hurried toward him, looking at him and nowhere else.

They'd agreed this morning that if he pulled his truck up to the curb, it meant he thought it was safe for her to come outside, he'd already checked. Their deal was, she wouldn't look around, wouldn't act scared, wouldn't tip off Asael that they were on to him. And she did all that, sold the shit out of her have-no-care-in-the-world vibe. She would make a good undercover officer, he thought.

She reached his car and slipped into the passenger seat. "Hey. Thanks for picking me up."

She smelled like pie and coffee, making Murph's mouth water. He'd missed her company all day. Being with her made his heart feel lighter. Okay, a pretty fanciful thought. Maybe Robin was rubbing off on him. *Love dove. Christ, that woman.*

He flashed a *friendly* smile at Kate. "Have a good day?"

"Not bad for an average Thursday. Two tour buses. Good tippers. You?"

"I got some work done at home. Reinforced doors, front, back and basement entry. Installed new heavy-duty locks."

"And if Asael doesn't hit at home?"

"I checked what information I could find on his work. He doesn't like an audience. He thinks himself to be invisible. Smoke. He likes hitting people when they least expect it, when their guards are down, on their own territory. But just in case." He jerked his thumb toward the backseat, the bulletproof vest he'd grabbed from the station. "I want you to wear Kevlar under your clothes. It's the latest technology, not too thick. It's winter anyway; everybody's bulky."

She raised an eyebrow.

Right. "Not you." He backpedaled. "Even in the

thickest sweater, you're as slim as a monk's chance for getting laid."

She laughed out loud. "Nice save."

"I want to ask you to consider something," he said as he turned down their street. "I want to bring at least the captain in on this."

Her eyes snapped wide, hands coming up to ward off the very idea. "No."

"He can help. I trust the man with my life."

"I don't trust him with mine. I don't know him. As far as I'm concerned, the only reason I'm still alive is because up until now, nobody knew my secret. Don't make me regret that I told you." She dropped her hands. "Please."

He stopped for a second at the stop sign and looked at her hands now tightly clasped on her lap, the stubborn set of her jaw. "I would feel better with Bing and the guys at the department having our back."

"If Asael has been watching the town for a few days now, he might notice any unusual police activity. He'd be tipped off that we're on to him. He might back off, but he'll never give up. He can't afford to let me live." She sounded exhausted, as if she'd already thought this over a dozen times, a hundred.

"Okay. You're right." He wasn't going to argue with her. He was going to help her. If Asael figured out they were onto him, he'd be a lot more careful, more difficult to trap. He might wait until Kate moved on, was on her own again.

"I won't tell Bing. For now." Murph tapped the break to turn onto his street. "We'll see how much we can accomplish today, how comfortable we feel with what we have."

Her Chevy was parked off to the side of his driveway, so he pulled into his garage. That shouldn't seem suspicious. The weather was plenty cold outside.

By the time he closed the garage door, she was checking out the security system on the wall. "Looks complicated."

"Not really. The code is *bonbons.*" He demonstrated. "So the chocolate hoarders among us can remember it."

He kept finding stashes of chocolate in the oddest places. Who kept truffles in the laundry cabinet?

"I don't know what you're talking about." But she smiled as she stepped inside the laundry room and looked around. "You've accessorized."

"A little." He'd put up a fire extinguisher, left a broom leaning against the wall a few feet farther in. "I tried to make sure you have something that can be used as a weapon close at hand, no matter where you are."

"Very safe-house chic. But I'm not planning on putting my gun down until this is over." She pulled the small weapon from her purse, checked to make sure that the safety was on, then shoved it into the back of her waistband in a move she'd probably seen on TV.

All that tough-chick stuff looked damn sexy on her.

Murph's gaze ran down her long legs. *Patience. Keep her safe first, seduce her second.* He wanted her, but that would have to wait. Maybe, in the meanwhile, he'd grow on her. He didn't think the chemistry he felt was one-sided.

He followed her in. "I don't suppose the gun shop threw in some training with that weapon."

"Bought it off the Internet. Watched YouTube videos on how to shoot, then practiced aiming, unloaded. I thought that would be safest."

He shook his head as he walked into the kitchen, feeling a headache coming on. He rubbed the heel of his hand against his temple. As an officer of the law, he wasn't the biggest fan of Internet weapons sales.

"We'll train. I'll take you to the shooting range. But any weapon can be taken away and turned against you. Any weapon can fail. It's good to have backup. We'll do a walk-through, so you can memorize the house. Then tonight we'll walk through again in the dark a couple of times. I want you to know where every door is, every item that you can use to defend yourself, even if you can't see them."

Kate swallowed as she tossed her purse on the hall table that held the mail, then dropped onto the couch, on the opposite end from his rolled-up bedding. She kicked off her sneakers and flexed her toes. "How soon do you think he'll come?"

"If we don't tip him off that we're onto him, soon. He found you. He knows where you live. He's watched the house, knows the parameters, probably made his plans. He has no reason to linger. He'll come at night, maybe make the hit look like a botched robbery."

Murph paused, leaning against the counter as he watched her, worry rising up hard in his stomach. "Or make it look like I snapped. Murder-suicide. Since he doesn't have a client to request the hit to be done this way or that, he'll go with what's cleanest. Whatever is the easiest for the authorities to digest. He wouldn't want an extensive investigation, anything to point to him. He's never been caught. His record is everything to him. The man didn't name himself Devil Smoke for nothing."

Kate rolled her ankles as she considered his words.

He tried not to stare at her endless legs. He pushed away from the counter, stopping as a stray thought popped into his head. "What if you know him?"

Her head snapped up. "What?"

"If he's been in town for a while, stalking you… What if he got in touch, like some sick game? To get to know you better."

"I would recognize him."

"You said that he disguised himself at the funeral. He could be in disguise here." Murph considered the possibility for a few seconds. "A guy new to town, someone who moved here after you did. Who do you know like that?"

She stared at him with a skeptical look on her face. She probably thought he'd just flipped. But then she said, "Jimmy Masters. He helps out in the kitchen at the diner. He was hired two days after I was. But he's *not* Asael."

"He ever tried to get you alone?"

"I'm helping him study for his GED." She hesitated. "Actually, tomorrow we'll be having our lesson at his apartment."

"No."

"This is crazy. He's way too young."

"Who else?"

"Nobody." But then she said, "Fred Kazincky. The mechanic who works on my car. He's older than Asael. And shorter, okay? I don't think that can be faked." She paused. "The dark blue sedan that I thought might be following me, that happened on my way to Fred. And he was right there in the shop, had been there, working on my car. It's not Fred."

"Okay." But Murph made a note of the name and was going to run him through the system at the station anyway.

She got up and went around him to the fancy hot chocolate machine she'd brought home from the diner. She hadn't tested it yet, but he'd caught her, on more than one occasion, casting longing glances that way.

"I'm making a cup. If we're having this conversation, I need a little something," she said, the way Murph's father used to talk about hard liquor. She pulled the machine to the middle of the counter. Then she froze, her gaze snapping to Murph. "Antonio."

"Who's that?"

"The chocolate salesman who gave me this. He got Southeastern PA as his sales territory around the same time that I moved here. I was already at the diner when he first came in. Then he became a regular."

Murph strode up to the machine and gently pushed her aside. "Hold on."

He looked at the shiny contraption from every angle. With way too many buttons and levers, the appliance looked unnecessarily complicated and expensive.

He disliked the idea of some strange guy giving Kate gifts. He wanted to know why. Because he was a cop. Not because he was jealous. Okay, because he was jealous.

"Have you two been involved?"

"None of your business."

"Want to stay alive?"

She glared at him. "He's not a killer. He's Italian."

"Right. Because an accent can't be faked." He scowled at the machine. "Don't touch this."

He hurried down to the basement and returned with his red toolbox, weighing his chances of being able to talk Kate into quitting work.

"What if you stayed home for a while?" he asked as he set the toolbox on the counter and opened it.

She cast a worried look at the contents. "Because that wouldn't look suspicious. What are you doing?"

He pulled her new toy closer. "Looking for a hidden camera or a mike."

Or a poison capsule.

Her eyes narrowed. "If you break my hot chocolate machine, I'm never forgiving you."

A risk Murph was willing to take. However, taking the machine apart piece by piece netted him no extra components, no surveillance equipment, no poison.

He put the damn thing back together, then slid it toward her on the counter. "See? No screws left over. Good as new."

She pushed the contraption into the far corner, moving the toaster in front of it for protection.

He held up a hand. "I'll leave it alone. I swear." Paused. "Anyone else?"

"No. I haven't been here long enough to make that many friends."

He caught an odd change in her tone. Regret? It couldn't be easy living on the run. No family, and no friends either, because she couldn't afford to let anyone too close, could she? And even if she got to know someone, soon she had to leave them behind.

The last of Murph's misgivings about taking on Asael evaporated with that thought. Kate deserved a better life.

"A lot of people come into the diner," he said. "Any regulars?"

"Our regulars are long-term locals. I don't think Asael is from Broslin."

Murph wasn't willing to write off the possibility as easily as that, but, in his heart of hearts, he didn't think so either. From what he'd learned of Asael from the various law enforcement databases, he was a man of the world with multiple secret residences all over the globe. Law enforcement had a list of suspected cities but hadn't yet been able to track down any of his lairs.

"I grew up here." He'd gone to school with a lot of the people who were around his age, like Asael was suspected to be. "Can't think of anyone in town who could lead that kind of double life without being missed while he's off doing evil in the world for weeks at a time, setting up jobs, then executing elaborate plans.

Kate nodded. "I'm going to change out of my work clothes."

She headed toward the bedroom, abandoning the hot chocolate machine, as if Murph had spoiled it for her.

He hadn't meant to do that.

Frustration cut through him.

Their relationship was getting more complicated by the minute. He needed to take it back to the basics. First and foremost, he wanted to protect her from a killer.

"Change into something you can move in. We're going to train."

CHAPTER FIFTEEN

Kate grunted as they lay in a tangle of limbs on the living room floor. She was so aware of Murph's chiseled body touching hers, she was ready to jump out of her skin. Half her body ached from the training session; the other half tingled with the kind of desire she'd just about forgotten.

She pulled back to put some distance between them. "Sorry. I'm not normally this uncoordinated."

He rolled away, keeping his bad shoulder protected, then pushed fluidly to his feet and stood there, looking down at her, not even breathing hard, the bastard.

She scrambled up as gracefully as a newborn foal on ice, doing her best to catch her breath. "I should start dinner."

"Let's try one more time." He moved toward her. "Pretend I'm the assassin. Murph is dead in the kitchen. You're out of bullets and cornered." He reached for her. "First choice?"

"Kill the bastard." She grabbed for the bar stool and whacked him over the head as hard as she could, but he twisted at the last second, and the blow glanced off his skull.

Right at the beginning, he'd ordered her to hold

nothing back. And then he'd pushed and pushed, baiting and goading her. At this stage, if she maimed him, she figured he deserved it.

"Second choice?" He stepped forward with a growl.

"Incapacitate him, then call 911." She lunged forward instead of pulling back, and kicked at his most sensitive parts, but wobbled at the last second and missed by a fraction of an inch.

"Third choice?" He grabbed for her.

"Run like hell and live to see another day." She was panting as she put her head down, then yanked it up hard, smashing it into his chin so that his head snapped back and his grip on her slipped.

She ran for the stairs that led up to the unfinished bedrooms.

He was on top of her in a second, bringing her down and pinning her. "Wrong move. What did I say about the stairs?"

"If I have a choice, go down." The basement had an outside exit, but upstairs she could get trapped.

"Right." He rolled off her, then sat on the bottom step, his eyes narrowing as he watched her struggle to catch her breath.

His biceps bulged under his black T-shirt that was barely wrinkled, while her shirt and pants looked like he'd mopped the house with her. Which, technically, he had.

She lay on the floor, gathering the strength to stand. He was insanely strong. She hadn't expected that, considering his injury. And he was fast. He didn't have to think about what move he was going to make next. He fought on instinct, while *her* instincts pushed her to run away screaming.

Except when they pushed her to throw herself into his arms. She looked away from him, not wanting him to read her pitiful reaction in her eyes.

He reached for her hand and helped her sit up. "I'm going to reinforce the rain spouts. Then, if you have no other choice, you can go upstairs and climb down without breaking your neck."

"I can break my neck even if the rain spout doesn't give out under me. I'm not a circus acrobat."

He closed his eyes for a second. "All right. If at all possible, go for the basement." He pulled a set of car keys from his pocket and handed it to her.

"What are these for?"

"A rented black Mustang, parked in front of 212 Summer Lane. You run out the basement door, cross the back neighbors' yard. I left money and a backup gun in the glove compartment. If all else fails, you jump in and drive away. Tank is full. Just drive and be safe."

"And you?"

"Don't worry about me."

Tension filled the air between them as they stared at each other. Her gaze dipped to his lips. She wanted him to kiss her again. She wrote that down to the post-fight adrenaline rush, because she didn't want to think about the alternative, that she wanted and liked him for real. She so wasn't in a place in her life where she could contemplate a relationship. "I don't want you to get hurt."

"We're going up against a professional hit man. We're going to get hurt. Our best-case scenario is just not to be dead when this is over."

She drew back. The idea of being free of Asael drew her irresistibly. She would have given just about anything for that kind of freedom. But she wouldn't give Murph.

"Maybe we shouldn't do this. I can just leave. I'm good at running. I'm a hell of a lot better at running than I am at fighting." Her thoughts were spinning in circles. There was so much at stake.

"If all goes well, you won't have to fight. I'll fight for you. Unless you want to turn yourself in to the FBI, ending the chase here and now is your best chance. You have a partner this time, someone who's been trained both as a cop and a soldier. And we know Asael is coming. He lost the element of surprise."

She gave a hesitant nod. "It's one of those now-or-never things isn't it?'

"We'll set the trap for the day after tomorrow. I don't want to wait too long, or he might make his move when we're not expecting him."

She drew a deep breath. "Okay. Let's do it."

"We'll make a show of me leaving. But I'll circle back and come in through the back door. When he comes, I'll engage him. If he gets through me, you run for your life. But it's not going to happen. I'm going to handle him."

Murph stood, then reached out and pulled her to her feet.

She hesitated a moment before she asked, "How is your shoulder?"

"What shoulder?"

"You favor your left side. I know you're still hurting."

"I can use my arm." As if to prove it, he reached up with his left and put a hand under her chin, tilting her face to him.

She swayed closer, then closer yet. "Murph."

He lowered his head to hers and kissed her.

Everything went still inside her as his warm lips touched hers. *Sweet chocolate mocha mousse saints.* She hadn't realized how much she'd missed this, a man's arms around her, his dark gaze boring into hers with scorching heat. And, boy, could Murph Dolan fix a girl with a look that sent tingles all the way down to her toes.

He smelled like man, tasted like coffee, and felt like heaven.

Her eyelids fluttered closed, and she gave herself to the sensation of being pressed against his hard chest while his mouth explored hers gently, teasing her, tasting her. His great warrior body vibrated with restrained need, but he didn't rush the kiss.

He brushed his lips over hers in agonizingly slow motion, covering every nook and cranny, then catching her bottom lip between his teeth for a second before he swept inside and tasted her fully, making her weak in the knees.

He gathered her against him tightly, chest to chest, hip to hip. She wouldn't have minded staying there forever.

"I wanted to do this from the moment I saw you sleeping in my bed," he murmured against her mouth.

"I just wanted to shoot you." She said the first thing that popped into her dazed mind.

He laughed as he stepped back. "That's a very healthy survival instinct. We're going to develop more of that in what little time have."

And then he attacked her.

* * *

He had to go back to the fighting before he did something stupid like scoop her up and carry her off to the bedroom. The thought that she was sleeping in his bed teased Murph every night, leaving him tossing and turning on the couch.

"Come on, like you mean it. Like you just caught me raiding your chocolate stash," he egged her on, knowing they didn't have nearly enough time for her to receive the training she needed.

She tried to punch him in the nose, missed and punched him in the mouth. Definitely not a trained fighter, but she was quick, and stronger than she looked. She was so bad with the fighting, really, that she was unpredictable, never doing what someone more seasoned would do. Which could work in her favor.

"If I'm out of commission for some reason, and you're out of bullets," he said, "then deflect and retreat, deflect and retreat. The mission objective changes to escape and evasion at that point. You're not going to take him out in hand-to-hand combat."

She did as he told her. When he moved in to grab her, she deflected his hands with a couple of well-aimed chops, then retreated. Then tripped on the rug in the back hallway, teetered backward, overcorrected and ended up falling forward into his arms.

Note to self: remove all area rugs.

She stared up at him with her sparkling-sky eyes.

He wanted to kiss her again. His body hummed with lust. Touching her did things to him, and would be best avoided, but he couldn't very well train her without touching. He wanted to kiss her and not stop this time. He wanted to go way past kissing. He wanted those longs legs of hers wrapped around his waist. He wanted to be so deep inside her tight heat—

He clenched his jaw.

Not yet.

When she was safe.

CHAPTER SIXTEEN

Murph was going to kiss her again. Kate wanted him to. He dipped his head toward hers, but then he pulled up the last second before they could touch lip to lip.

"We have work to do," he whispered into her hair.

That was what romance novels meant when they mentioned *strangled whisper*, she thought, her entire body alive and buzzing.

She took a reluctant step back, then another, toward the kitchen. He was right. For one, she needed to start dinner. She needed a break from training, from the overwhelming sexual tension between them that was leaving her breathless.

"I'll make a couple of Philly cheese steaks," she said as the gears in her brain began turning again. "I brought fresh rolls home from the diner. They were baked just before I left."

He gave her a smile as if she were an angel come to earth. "You fix the cheese steaks, and I'll go and work on reinforcing the rain spouts. Since there's ice hanging off the gutters, it shouldn't look suspicious if I go out there with a ladder and start cleaning up a little."

The idea of her climbing out an upstairs window and gliding down the drainpipe to the ground made her queasy, so she turned to the kitchen to occupy herself with things she could actually handle.

She began chopping the onions while Murph shrugged into his coat and stepped into black boots. He was out the door by the time she remembered that it might be difficult for him to climb the ladder while carrying tools, then try to work—all that with only one good shoulder.

She turned off the stove and began walking after him to offer help, but then stopped. He'd resent it. He wore his can-do Army attitude like armor. He wasn't afraid of anything.

Then again, she was plenty scared for the both of them. As he'd said, there was a good chance for one or both of them getting hurt here. She was a target. She'd lived with that for eighteen months now. But she didn't want him hurt because, honestly, this had nothing to do with him. Asael wasn't his problem. Murph getting hurt was just as unacceptable as her parents or her sister getting hurt. She cared about Murph.

That admission knocked Kate back a step.

Because she cared about him *a lot*.

More than what was smart?

She went back to the stove, turned it on, and stirred the onions more forcefully than she had to. When they were sautéed, in just a minute, she set them aside and dropped the razor-thin slices of frozen beef into the pan.

She wasn't the type to fall in love in the blink of an eye. She wasn't the type to fall in love at all. In all her previous relationships, she always held back, took forever to trust, then was never able to give herself fully. *Never.*

She could definitely not be falling in love in the middle of all this mess.

No, she was just confused. All the pressure and danger were messing with her head.

So when they had dinner later, sitting across the table

from each other, she kept her mental distance as best she could. And when Murph looked at her, really looked at her—God, the man knew how to look at a woman with his dark-chocolate eyes so she felt it all the way down to her toes—she looked away.

Keeping aloof was more difficult once they were at the indoor shooting range where he drove her—careful to make sure they weren't followed—after they ate.

Two dozen well-lit lanes, about a dozen people, most of whom turned to the newcomers as they walked in.

"Murph!"

"You're back!"

"Good to see you, buddy."

Almost everyone had something to say to him, followed by manly back clapping, except for the graying woman behind the counter, who ran around to give him a big hug. "You were in my prayers every night."

He hugged her back, unembarrassed. "They made a difference, Dottie." Then he pulled away. "This is my friend, Kate. I brought her by for some practice."

"Fun date." Dottie looked Kate over. "He's never brought a girl here before. You must be special, honey. Some men don't like their women having a good aim. They might get shot in the ass, if they step out of line, if you know what I mean."

A man walked up from behind them, clapped Murph on the shoulder, then raised his hands. "Not the wandering kind." He kissed Dottie as he passed her on his way behind the counter. Got everything I need right at home. Luckiest son of a gun in the world."

Dottie grinned, obviously pleased, and went to join the man Kate assumed was her husband. "Dave here will set you up, honey. Then Murph will take good care of you. Let's just fill out the paperwork."

They were a cute couple. Kate didn't correct the date assumption—reality being too complicated to explain. She just listened to the safety instructions, and signed on the dotted lines.

Ten minutes later, all set up, the butterflies in her stomach were having a ball as she tried to aim at the bull's-eye, doing her best to ignore Murphs firm chest pressed against her back, his muscular arms around her as he showed her how to properly handle her weapon.

Since they were touching again, she was all tingly and distracted. He even smelled like a warrior, his masculine scent mixing with the smell of metal and gunpowder.

"Focus," he yelled to be heard over all the shots going off around them.

She ignored the other shooters and lined up her sights, both hands on the gun. When she squeezed the trigger, his support helped her arms absorb the weapon's kick.

He pulled back, giving her space to do it again and again, on her own this time. Her focus improved tremendously.

She emptied the magazine, then they waited until the pulley brought the target up to them, the black outline of the upper body of a man with circles painted on him. Nerves grabbed hold of her suddenly. She wanted to do well. This was important. She wanted to prove to Murph that she was up to the challenge before them.

"Not bad."

The holes were grouped roughly in the middle.

"Not bad at all." Murph smiled, and she was ridiculously pleased by the impressed look on his face. "Actually, pretty good for an amateur. Ever thought about joining law enforcement?"

"I'm not sure they're the best match for my skillset. Do police officers give massages?"

He cracked up. "The images you're putting in my head." He rubbed his eyes with his knuckles. "Now how am I going to unsee that?"

Dottie behind the counter saw them having fun and winked at Kate.

While Murph said, "All right. Back to work."

He gave her some tips, then made her practice for another hour.

She was mentally exhausted by the time they finished, but better. More accurate and faster. Practicing with real bullets was a big improvement over aiming an empty gun at her own reflection in the mirror.

Murph drove them home and parked in the garage again. He disarmed the security system, but when Kate reached for the light switch in the laundry room as she stepped inside, he put a hand over hers. "Now we learn the house blind."

He made her walk through in the dark, staying a step behind her.

"Note the fire extinguisher." And then, "Broom is to your right."

Next, he guided her to the kitchen knives, then to the living room.

"The reading lamp is heavy enough to be used as a weapon," he said, close to her ear, then he made her find, by feel, all the spots where his guns were hidden throughout the house.

She stubbed her toes and scraped her knuckles half a dozen times, at least, but she was pretty happy with herself.

She turned to him in the barely there moonlight. "I can do this."

"Not fast enough. Let's go through it again. With some speed." He was merciless.

He made her walk through faster. Then he made her run, in the dark, up and down the stairs, dashing around doorways.

"Who needs Asael? The training is going to kill me," Kate grumbled as she gasped for air at the end.

And then Murph attacked her.

He knocked her back, taking her by surprise. She fought like hell, punched, kicked, bit—or tried to. He twisted away from her, but her next punch landed. And she realized the dark gave her some advantage: since he couldn't see where she was looking, he couldn't anticipate her next move.

Somehow, by some miracle, she managed to trip him. As he stumbled back, she plowed head down into his solar plexus. They ended up on the floor, with her on top, straddling him. She twisted and fought to keep control, refusing to let him buck her off.

And then suddenly she felt something hard between her legs that wasn't his weapon.

Oh.

Oh!

They both stilled.

The next second, he flipped her, and in one smooth move rolled her under him. He kept most of his weight off her, pinning her down with his hands, his powerful thighs between hers.

Desire shot through her like lightning. Need clamored for fulfillment. God, it'd been a long time. *Forever.* And never with anyone who affected her like Murph did.

She wanted this. She wanted more. She wanted *him.*

A small sound escaped her throat, a moan of pure need.

He swore softly, then his lips were on hers. He tasted her as if she were made of the finest Swiss chocolate. The man was thorough in everything he did. First her training, and now her ravishing.

His mouth was a lethal weapon as he teased her, tortured her, brought her to capitulation. She was close to begging by the time he finally deepened the kiss. And then he took his time conquering her tongue, her mouth, her soul.

She slipped her hands under his shirt, and her fingers had a field day on his back, exploring shifting muscles and his warm, smooth skin.

His mouth left hers, but, before she could protest, his seeking lips found the curve of her neck. His five-o'clock shadow scraped against her sensitized skin, leaving nerve endings tingling in its wake. His left hand tightened on her hip, then his grip loosened as his palm traveled up until his long fingers covered her breast.

Holy mocha truffles.

She arched into his caresses.

Then he shifted and tugged, and her shirt disappeared. Urgent kisses outlined her bra; hot lips looked for entry. He found it pretty fast, peeling the bra down and licking his way across her skin.

When Murph sucked her nipple into his mouth, moisture gathered between Kate's thighs. Her eyes fluttered closed as exquisite sensations skittered through her. Her entire body buzzed by the time he moved on to the other nipple.

And when he tortured that, too, into a throbbing nub of pleasure, he moved lower.

She was ready for him, barely hearing the front door rattle.

He did. He stiffened—beyond the part that was already Olympic gold-medal stiff—and raised his head.

"Yoo-hoo! I saw you come home," Wendy White, the new neighbor shouted through the door. "I brought over some cookies."

Kate groaned, red hot frustration washing over her, pushing aside the red hot need.

Murph laid his head on her belly, breathing hard, holding on to her tightly. His voice was a hoarse whisper as he asked, "What are we doing here?"

"If I have to draw a map…" she joked, but neither of them were laughing.

He held her for another moment before he rolled off her with a groan, and she scrambled up on shaky legs, looking for her clothes in the dark so she could go and deal with the neighbor. Which took a lot longer than she'd expected.

Wendy wanted to stay and chat, and insisted on them listening to her nephew's songs she played on her phone at top volume. The boy was a new pop singer, sure to be the next big thing.

Kate was supportive and wished the nephew the best, she really did. But she so wasn't in the mood to entertain Wendy. She needed alone time to figure out what had just happened between her and Murph.

That Murph was shooting her undecipherable looks didn't help any. They made her twitchy. Because, try as she might, she couldn't make out if those looks meant *stay tuned for more*, or *this has been a mistake.*

CHAPTER SEVENTEEN

Murph looked at the fresh snow through the windshield as he drove Kate to work Friday morning. Nobody strayed outside unless in a well-heated car, the sidewalks empty. He didn't comment on the weather. He didn't comment on anything. He was going to keep his damn distance. He couldn't let his guard down again like he had the night before. Kate's life depended on him keeping vigilant and not getting distracted.

"I appreciate the ride," she said, watching him.

She hadn't brought up his lapse of judgment, and no way was he going to approach the subject. He couldn't talk sex with Kate. Not without wanting to do it.

After his new neighbor had left the night before, he'd taken a long cold shower, then turned in. He hadn't slept much, but at least he'd kept his hands off Kate, which was an accomplishment. Freaking medal-worthy.

"Remember where all the guns are in the house?" He spoke for the first time since they'd gotten into the car.

"Yes."

He glanced at her. "Prove it."

She rolled her eyes, but then she told him, exactly.

Fine. "You have the Kevlar on?"

She pulled her coat apart and her shirt collar down a little to show him.

"Key to the Mustang?"

"In my pocket," she said.

When they reached the diner, he went in with her to check out her workplace and the people who surrounded her during the day. For over an hour, he watched everyone who came near her, but none of the customers acted suspiciously, so he strode out and around.

A scrawny twenty-something in a blue apron was having a smoke in the back parking lot.

"Hey."

"Hey."

"Murph. Kate's friend. You must be Jimmy." He wanted to get a feel for him, even if he did appear too young to be Asael—Murph had to agree with Kate on that.

Jimmy nodded and offered him a smoke.

"No, thanks. Yours?" Murph nodded toward the beat-up Camaro next to the kid. The hood was a different color, the front bumper mostly missing, no hubcaps. And Murph had a feeling those were just the beginning of the vehicle's problems.

"Been fixing it up." Jimmy puffed out his chest. "Z28, 35th Anniversary Edition. Traded it for a broken phone."

Murph quirked an eyebrow.

"Broken screen. Customer came in, while he had his coffee and pie, he popped his SIM and SD cards into a new phone he got down the street, tossed the cracked one. Buddy of mine fixes cracked screens. He hates to get dirty. Prissy." Jimmy snorted. "I changed the oil in his car. He fixed the screen. I traded the phone online for a tablet with a cracked screen. Fixed that, traded it for a broken PC. It just needed a working fan." Jimmy shrugged. "I got one out of a computer they tossed over at the office park. Traded the PC online." Jimmy shrugged again. "Kept going."

Kid might have been a busboy, but he was no dummy,

Murph thought, and for a moment considered the difference between him and Robbie, and Robbie's idiot crew who lurked on street corners, looking for trouble, because they were bored.

The PD retired equipment from time to time: old printers and broken scanners and the like. Murph made a mental note to ask Leila to keep Jimmy in mind instead of setting anything reusable out with the trash.

"Are you going to trade the Camaro when it's finished?"

"No, man." Jimmy pulled back as if offended. "That's forever. She just needs some loving care."

Murph nodded. "Good luck. She's fine piece of machinery."

"Thanks." Jimmy puffed his cigarette to the filter, then hurried back to work.

Since the kid wasn't putting out any murderous vibes, Murph left the diner and drove to Arnie's Gas Station that had a mechanic shop attached to the back. It'd been a while since he'd last been there. He usually took his truck to Billy Pickett, who needed the money to support a big family depending on him.

Murph pulled up to the first free pump to fill his car, washed the windows, taking his time so he could catch a glimpse of Fred Kazincky.

Older guy. Greasy overalls. He seemed to know his way under the hood, worked hard and didn't lollygag around like some of the younger mechanics did.

According to Kate, he was shorter than Asael and couldn't have been in the dark sedan that had followed her, so Murph didn't spend a lot of time on him.

Before he headed home, he called Kate. "I want you to give me a ring if Antonio comes in."

"He's not Asael." She sounded breathless. They must have gotten busy.

"Call me anyway." After having seen Jimmy and Fred, Antonio was on the top of Murph's suspect list. "What's his last name?"

"I don't know."

"You could look it up on the credit card receipt."

"He usually pays cash."

"Another strike against him."

"Fine. I'll call. I have to go. This place is hopping."

Hearing her voice and picturing her running around in her little skirt brought the previous night to mind, and Murph was hot and bothered all over again by the time he reached the house, so he decided to work off his frustrations.

By noon the place was as fortified as he could make it without installing bulletproof windows and a machine-gun nest on the roof. Among other things, he'd reframed the laundry chute that went from the upstairs bathroom to the laundry room downstairs. It wasn't wide enough for him, but Kate could drop down without trouble if she got trapped upstairs. That route would be safer than her negotiating the rain spout outside.

Satisfied with the new security measures, he drove to the station for another look at the law enforcement databases.

Everybody was in.

"Slow day for crime in Broslin?" Murph asked as he walked through the door.

"And may it last. I'll put on a fresh pot of coffee for you," Leila smiled at him then headed for the back, wearing bright purple boots that matched her shirt.

Bing came out of his office. "Everything all right?"

"Just want to check on something. Mind if I sign into the system?"

"Go ahead. Anything I can help you with?"

Murph shook his head. "Tenant stuff. Anything I can help *you* with?" He didn't specify, but they both knew he meant Stacy's case.

"Nothing we can do without new leads," Bing said with the weariness of a man who'd been up all night again.

"So Kate is still living with you?" he asked, transparent in his need to change the subject.

"She's fine where she is," Murph told him, because as police captain, Bing sometimes handled evictions, and Murph had a feeling he was about to offer his assistance in that capacity. "I don't mind helping her out."

"Is she in some kind of trouble?"

Murph hesitated. He didn't want to lie. "Not with the law."

The captain stood in silence for a minute, then nodded, catching that it was Kate's private business, something Murph wasn't authorized to share.

"You can handle a nasty ex," he said at last, guessing at the nature of her difficulties. "But you know you only have to call if you want us to take care of it."

"I appreciate that."

Leila came from the break room with a steaming mug of coffee. She handed the mug to Murph as she picked up the ringing phone. "One minute, please," she said into the receiver, then put the call on hold and turned to Bing. "FBI is on line one, Captain. It's about the bank robberies."

Bing nodded at Murph then walked away, calling over his shoulder, "Let me know if you need anything else."

Murph thanked Leila for the coffee then headed back to his desk and plopped down in front of his computer, turned it on.

Chase was on the phone but waved at him.

Harper lifted a mocking eyebrow. "What are you doing here? Leggy redhead didn't work out? Too much for you, old man?"

Murph was two years older than Harper, a chasm. In maturity, in any case. "I can handle whatever comes my way, buddy."

"Oh yeah? Then why aren't you at home with her?"

"She's at work."

"How hot is she? Seriously."

Murph said nothing as he logged in.

Harper grabbed his chest. "That hot? Oh man. Can't believe she just fell into your bed. How come she decided to stay?"

"Women can't walk away from me. Watch and learn, kid."

Harper gave him the one-finger salute, then Leila transferred a call to him, so he had to pick up the phone.

Murph shook his head and pulled his keyboard closer. He looked up Rauch Asael again to see if any new information had been added.

He scanned the few new lines of data. According to the Interpol, there was some indication that at least on two separate occasions, Asael might have worked with an unidentified partner slash *love interest.*

Who the hell was that, and why hadn't she been mentioned before?

Murph set aside his questions and read the only other bit of new information.

The FBI had reason to believe that Asael was staying in Hong Kong as recently as this past Monday.

Murph had returned home on Monday. He'd seen someone in a dark blue sedan down the street from his house. If Asael had been in Hong Kong, who was watching Kate here? Who drove the dark blue sedan?

Asael's lover?

He tried to imagine two assassins as a pair of lovebirds. Like how police officers sometimes married other police officers. A lot of people met their significant others through the job. It even had a name: office romance.

Maybe assassins hooked up with other assassins. What the hell did he know about it? He read the report over again. The thought that Asael's lover might be in Broslin wouldn't let him rest.

Murph didn't think Asael would delegate this particular hit, not something this personal. Then again, maybe his lover took it upon herself to take Kate out.

The lover could be Delia, the new waitress at the diner,

or Murph's new neighbor, Wendy White, or any number of women. The damn report had nothing that could identify Asael's love interest. He opened the attached file.

The crime scene photos from Hong Kong mostly showed body parts. Murph's stomach turned. Hell, he could smell the blood. And the smoke. And then, the next second, Murph could hear his teammates screaming as the IEDs exploded. And just like that, he was back in the dry riverbed, the sun beating down on him as he scrambled half-blind to save his men.

He gritted his teeth, clenching and unclenching his hands, focusing on the room around him to shake off the flashback. Every muscle tense, his breath came in ragged gasps.

He closed the file, brimming with frustration as he ran background checks on Jimmy and Antonio next. Because, technically, Asael's lover could be either sex. Murph wasn't ruling out anything at this stage. On second thought, he also ran a background check on Fred the mechanic.

The men all checked out, nothing suspicious in the system. Of course, a professional assassin could fake a better false identity than Kate had. Just because Murph hadn't found anything, it didn't mean one of Kate's new friends wasn't hiding a dark secret.

Next, he ran Wendy White. Squeaky clean. Kind of local, grew up in Avon Grove.

Murph called over to Leila. "Do you know the new waitress at the diner? Delia. What's her last name?"

"Parisi."

"Thanks." Murph ran her name through the system next.

She was from Trenton, New Jersey, had lived there all her life until now. High school dropout. Minor trouble with the law. She'd smoked pot in her younger days.

Annoyed that he hadn't gained more information, Murph shut down the computer. He glanced at the captain's office. The door stood open, but Bing was still on the phone, looking decidedly unhappy.

They could catch up later.

"Heading home," Murph told the others. "Try to stay out of trouble."

Chase was on the phone again so he just waved.

Harper said, "Tell your girl to come by for a visit when she's ready to move on to finer things. I'd be happy to show her the best of what Broslin has to offer."

Murph waved at him with his middle finger sticking out, then thanked Leila for the coffee and stepped outside. Robin was bringing the mail, practically flying up the walkway, bundled up against the cold and then some, barely a slice of her face showing.

"Behind schedule." She zipped by Murph. But a second later, she called back, making him turn. "Congratulations on your new thresher!" Then she disappeared inside the station.

She'd gone off the deep end, for real. As soon as Murph had a free hour, he was going to take her to the diner for some pie and coffee, have a long chat and figure out what was going on with her. If this was something like Alzheimer's, somebody needed to notice and help her deal with it.

The loud bang came just as he reached his car. He hit the ground, the smell of smoke and sulfur and the blood in his nose. For a second, he heard the screams, and his heart slammed so hard against his rib cage he thought it might burst.

Then his vision cleared, and he could see the metal dumpster the truck across the street had accidentally dropped. The chains dangled from the lever as the driver jumped from the cab, swearing as he rushed back to see what had gone wrong.

Murph straightened. Clenched his jaw. Dusted off his pants.

He didn't look around to see if anyone had witnessed his idiocy. He got into his car and slammed the door shut.

Swore.

His breathing harsh, his muscles stiff, he just sat for a moment as a dark mood descended on him. So this was a first. Maybe *he* was going nuts. Maybe he was worse off than he'd thought. Maybe he shouldn't have talked Kate into staying.

What if I can't protect her?

Long seconds passed before he could push that thought away. Doubts were the enemy. A successful op had no room for that kind of crap. He'd protect her or die trying. Because he still believed Kate's best chance was staying with him.

He called her cell as he turned the key in the ignition. "The hit man might be a woman."

"What?"

"Asael was just in Hong Kong. He sometimes works with a love interest of his. So if Asael isn't in Broslin, then the person watching you might be his lover. Are you at work?"

"Where else would I be?"

"Antonio?"

"Hasn't come in yet today."

"Keep an eye on the women too. Especially anyone new to town who's been acting friendly with you." The idea of her being surrounded by strangers, any one of whom could be the killer, had all his muscles tightening.

"Delia is here," she said after a moment.

"I'm heading over there right now." He hung up as he turned onto Main Street, into heavier traffic.

CHAPTER EIGHTEEN

Kate waited at the counter for Eileen to fill the coffee mugs for the table of older women on an antiquing trip. They were sweet, and cute, all seven wearing identical pink sweaters with their club's green logo in the middle.

Murph sat in the corner, his back to the wall, in a position from where he could see everything. He finally finished scrutinizing the employees and the current customers and was now staring individually at each new person who came in.

A thrill ran through Kate every time she looked at him, their tumble on the floor the night before playing on an endless loop in her mind. She'd nearly spilled the half-dozen strawberry milkshakes when she'd served the table next to his. Good thing they'd been super thick and could take a little extra jostling.

Murph gave no sign that he even remembered what the two of them had done in his foyer. He was definitely in a different mood. He brought a dark energy with him that didn't belong at the diner.

"Who's the new guy?" Kate asked Eileen, nodding toward the handsome stranger in the corner, the only person Murph hadn't scrutinized. He'd even given the man a friendly nod.

"Jack Sullivan. Might be joining the PD."

That explained it.

"Tall, dark, and handsome," Eileen's tone grew suggestive. "Hope he'll become a regular. Single women will be flocking in."

Not as handsome as Murph, Kate thought, and knew how lost she was. *Biased much?*

Sullivan was watching the customers almost as avidly as Murph. He sat with his back to the wall, his body language telegraphing *ready.*

For what?

A man with secrets. It took one to know one. Kate wondered if she looked like that at times, muscles forced to relax, but the eyes hyper-aware, always scanning.

To be fair, Sullivan was a lot more subtle about his surveillance of the diner than Murph. Eileen didn't seem to pick up on his vigilance, while she was watching Murph with a frown as she filled the last mug on the tray.

"How long is he going to stay?" she asked, just as Murph abruptly pushed to his feet and strode over to them.

He took the tray Kate had just picked up and set it back on the counter. "Kate is leaving early today," he told Eileen. "And she's not coming in tomorrow."

With that, he took Kate's hand and dragged her through the back, barely leaving her time to grab her purse. And she went along, gritting her teeth, only because she didn't want to cause a scene and make everything worse.

She dialed Eileen as soon as they were in the car, and Murph let her go. "I'm really sorry about that."

"Did he just snap? Should I call Bing? Are you okay?"

"I'm fine. I'm so sorry. I'll be at work tomorrow. I promise."

"Now that I've seen how he is, I don't like the idea of you living with him. That man needs help."

"I'm going to talk to him about that. I can handle this.

We're fine. I swear. I'm sorry."

There was a brief silence on the line. "All right. I can pick up the slack here until the second shift comes in. Call me if I can help with anything."

"Thank you, Eileen." She hung up, then turned to Murph, but he cut her off before she could give voice to the righteous anger bubbling up inside her.

"There was no way to keep you safe there. It's an unsecure location. I don't want you to go back."

"I wasn't alone, isolated. I was among people." She ground the words out through clenched teeth.

"And some of those people we know nothing about." He passed an Amish buggy that had three little kids in straw hats in the back. "Why didn't Antonio show?"

"He doesn't come every day." She wanted to talk to Antonio too, about that hot chocolate machine. She'd given Eileen some cash in an envelope to cover his next several meals. They didn't have the kind of relationship where she would have been comfortable accepting a gift that big.

"I don't appreciate caveman tactics, especially at my workplace," she told Murph. "I thought you said Asael would come at night. When you leave and he thinks I'm by myself. Isn't that his way?"

"Except it might be his lover coming for you. And while we know Asael's MO, we have no idea how his lover-disciple works. For all we know she's a sharpshooter who likes to take her victims in the middle of a crowd from a distance."

Despite the heater going full blast in the car, cold spread through her as she stared at Murph.

"You're scaring me."

Then again, to be fair, this whole situation scared her. Maybe she was just looking to blame her anxiety on someone. Still, bottom line, she didn't like the way he'd handled things at the diner. He looked strong and capable, but she knew where the cracks were. She knew he wasn't a hundred percent physically. And she wasn't sure if he was a hundred percent mentally either, if the danger with Asael was quite as clear and present as he said, or paranoia from the PTSD Murph denied having.

He was a warrior, but an injured warrior, with problems he refused to face.

"You *should* be scared," he said, his tone clipped. "This is not a game."

No, it wasn't.

She needed to accept some hard truths here. She liked Murph a lot. She wanted him to save her. But what if he couldn't? Maybe he couldn't even save himself at the moment, not until he faced his own issues.

The memory of him screaming in the night tore at her heart. He needed help, and not just with his arm but therapy for PTSD, possibly more surgeries, certainly physical therapy. He might look like the strongest man she'd ever met, but she was pretty sure he was broken in his hidden places.

Had some dark car on their street really been acting strangely the night he'd come home? Had someone really been inside the house? She'd seen no sign of an intruder. Yes, she thought she'd been followed once. But she could have been wrong. She hadn't seen that car since.

And then the whole Asael's lover angle… It seemed too far-fetched to Kate.

Maybe Murph felt guilty for losing his men and subconsciously thought he could redeem himself if he saved her.

"Have you scheduled your physical therapy yet with the VA?"

"When this is over," he said.

"So now what?" she asked with caution.

"Now we'll hole up in the house and set the trap."

"When"

"Tomorrow."

"And if he doesn't come?" What if no hit man or woman was in Broslin at all?

He rolled his good shoulder. "We wait. We stay ready."

"I could just disappear again." Suddenly, their plan to draw out Asael seemed a lot less solid than it had the day before. Kate wanted to go home to her family so badly, she would have considered anything that helped her do that, but she had to keep a clear head. "I could disappear tonight."

"No. We've been through this. Going on the road now would be too dangerous. You have to see this through. And the only way to see this through is the way we planned it. Make him think you're alone, then when he strikes, I move in and take care of him."

She had no idea what to do, what to tell Murph, so she stayed quiet for the rest of the trip home.

He pulled into the garage. "Don't get out until the door is all the way down."

They sat next to each other in tense silence, Murph's gaze fixed on the rearview mirror, until the edge of the garage door touched the cement floor with a rattle. Then they went into the house, Murph first, gun drawn as he disabled the security system. He armed it again behind them.

"Stay here." He moved forward to search the place and drew down the blinds as he went.

Sunlight disappeared little by little until they were left in near darkness, the house as gloomy as a crypt.

When he signaled to her, she moved into the kitchen. "Is this necessary?"

There was something spooky about the way he behaved, something unhealthy. She was familiar with behavior like this from abuse survivors. She'd been like this herself at one point—irrational and paranoid. She couldn't go back into that dark cave with him. He needed professional help. He needed more support than she could give right now, with the mess she was in.

His left arm twitched.

"You need rest," she said.

"I'll rest when it's over."

Her heart ached for him. They might both be good

people. They might even be right for each other, could be good for each other. But they'd met at the wrong time, with their lives at the wrong place.

Her presence here wasn't good for him—the thought hit her, and she couldn't deny it. She'd brought stress to his life. Danger. He needed the opposite.

Her phone rang.

"Don't answer. It might be tapped." His face was grim, his forehead drawn in concentration.

She glanced at the display. *Eileen.* The call could wait.

All Kate could think was that Murph looked like a man who'd just gone over the deep end. They both needed healing. He needed time, but her troubles kept him busy and preoccupied. She needed to leave so he could focus on getting better and reclaiming his old life.

She passed by him, heading down the hall. "I'm going to my room to change."

"Don't go near the window."

"I won't."

She closed the door behind her, changed her clothes, pulling on a comfortable pair of jeans and a soft T-shirt. She hesitated over the bulletproof vest that she'd worn all day under her uniform shirt. Did she really need that inside the house with Murph in the kitchen?

She didn't want to sink into paranoia all the way and get stuck in some dark place for the rest of her life. She took the vest and hung it in her closet.

As she moved the hangers aside, her purple Christmas sweater slid to the ground. She picked it up, slipped into it, then reached for her phone.

It might be tapped.

She was ninety-nine percent sure that Murph was wrong, but she sat down on the bed and reached into the nightstand's top drawer, anyway. She dug around for the disposable cell phone she kept there as backup, and when she found it, she pulled up the only number stored on it, the number she'd kept in case things ever careened completely out of control. She certainly felt like she had reached that point.

Either the killer was in town or not. Either Murph could protect her, or he'd gone completely over the edge. Kate had no idea what was the right move to make. She knew only one thing for sure: she wanted to live.

All right... She knew something else as well. She wanted Murph to be able to live fully and heal from his past, which would be impossible as long as she kept dumping her troubles on him.

She'd done well until now, on the run, but maybe this was as far as she could make it on her own. Maybe Murph was right. Maybe it was time for witness protection.

She had only three choices, really: gambling her life on her own sparse and questionable skills, or on Murph, who was broken, or trusting the professionals.

God, let this be the right decision, Kate thought as she pushed the button and called Agent Cirelli.

CHAPTER NINETEEN

Knowing that a killer had Kate in the crosshairs sent all of Murph's protective instincts rushing to the surface. He had just finished checking all the windows when she came back into the kitchen. The sight of her gave him a jolt as always. Her long legs were encased in slim jeans; on top she wore—

"What's that?" He stared at the orange reindeer on a wild purple background.

She touched a hand against it. "My lucky sweater. My sister made it for me for the last Christmas we had together. I had it on at the FBI stakeout, so it came with me."

He squinted. "Does Rudolph have an—"

"That's his other leg," she cut him off. "It's the first sweater Emma ever knitted. It's not perfect." She stuck her chin out as if daring him to say something about her sister's gift.

She was loyal. And beautiful, but his fascination with her went beyond that. She was warm, nice to people. He'd seen that at the diner. She was a hard worker. She was a genuinely good person, about as far from his mother as a woman could be, and nothing like Doug's wife either.

Murph actually *could* imagine a lifetime with someone like her.

She flashed a nervous smile, stopping a good distance from him. "I called the FBI."

He'd recommended that very thing to her, yet words felt like a slap across the face. His jaw snapped tight. "Why?"

"I think you were right at the beginning. This might be bigger than what the two of us can handle. Maybe I do need outside help."

His muscles tensed. More than *he* could handle, she meant. She didn't trust him, obviously, to keep her safe. "How soon will they be here?"

"A couple of hours? Agent Cirelli is driving up from DC."

Because Kate trusted Agent Cirelli more than she trusted Murph.

Murph wanted to punch something, even if he knew he was being damn unreasonable. The FBI would keep Kate safe. Wasn't that what he wanted?

She'd reached out—the right thing to do. Talking to Cirelli wasn't a betrayal in any way. Yet it felt like a rejection. He was damaged, the thought burned through him. He wasn't good enough anymore. Why would she want to trust her life to him?

He needed to walk away for a minute, needed to swallow the bitter taste that bubbled up his throat. He checked the gun in the back of his waistband. "I'm going to walk around the house. You stay in here."

She pressed her lips together. "I'm sorry, Murph."

He armed the security system then headed outside without glancing back. "You did the right thing."

He stopped on the front stoop, filling his lungs with cold air. He looked around, as if surveying what needed to be done around the house, in case anyone was watching.

The sky had turned winter gray, dark snow clouds hiding the sun. The temperature had dipped again, but at least the wind wasn't blowing. He headed around the side, walked into the garage from the back, and grabbed his shovel. Shoveling the driveway and the walkway to the front door would give him long enough to check out the neighbors and the street.

He would keep Kate safe until the FBI got there, a couple of hours. He was determined to do that, at least.

He was striding back up front with the shovel when he saw a shadow move in the window next door. *Wendy White.* Was she watching him? Was she Asael's lover? Was she hoping that Murph would leave?

The window she was standing behind faced Kate's bedroom. Could be a coincidence. Or not.

Had Wendy been spying on Kate all along?

Murph pushed the shovel into snow, and as he heaved the frozen slush to the side, he caught sight of Wendy shifting something long and slim and straight in her hands.

The brief glimpse he caught wasn't enough to tell whether it was a broom handle or the barrel of a rifle.

Oh hell. He reached for his gun, but she disappeared from sight the next second.

Wendy White.

She had no criminal record, but there was her odd visit with a plate of cookies the night before, the way she'd talked and talked, then the strange business with the music. Something was off there. She'd set off his cop instincts.

He glanced at his watch. According to Kate, Wendy went over to the diner for lunch every day around this time. That gave him an idea. Murph dropped his shovel, ducked between the bushes that separated the two properties and came out on the other side, pulled his pocketknife and ducked behind Wendy's old station wagon.

He had her license plate off in a second. He kicked it into the snow bank that edged her driveway, then hurried back and picked up the shoveling where he'd left off. No more than ten minutes passed before Wendy walked from her house to her car, then took off with a cheerful wave at him.

Murph dialed Harper at the station. "I've got a favor to ask. I need someone to pick up Wendy White for driving without a license plate. She's my new neighbor. She's heading to the Main Street Diner right now." He rattled off the make and model of her car and the exact color, forest green. "I need you to find a way to keep her awhile. Suspicion of being under the influence, refusing to cooperate with police, whatever you can make fly."

Silence stretched on the other end, then, "Want to tell me what this is about?"

Murph glanced toward his house. "I think Kate might be in serious danger."

"From your new neighbor?"

"Possibly. I'd appreciate it if you could run her prints."

"And then you're going to tell me what the hell is going on?"

"As soon as I can." Murph hung up and ducked back between the bushes, went around Wendy's house, checking the doors and windows—everything locked.

He walked to the back door of her garage, careful to keep under the eaves where there was no snow so he wouldn't leave telltale footprints. This door was locked too, but old enough so lifting the lock and wiggling it did the trick.

Murph stepped inside and scanned the cavernous, mostly empty space. The new neighbor hadn't lived in the house long enough to fill the garage to the rafters, just a few moving boxes lined up against the wall.

Murph cut straight to the door that led to the inside of the house. No alarm decal. He hadn't seen a sign up front that advertised a security company, either.

Here we go.

He pulled out his pocketknife and picked the lock.

Then he pushed the door open inch by slow inch, hoping he'd find proof that Wendy was connected to Asael. Because if the FBI arrested Wendy today, then Kate would be finally safe. And if she was safe, she wouldn't have to leave.

* * *

Kate packed her single suitcase, then decided to make a lasagna for Murph's freezer for when she was gone. She had some time before the FBI would arrive, and she needed to do something to keep busy, or she'd go nuts before Agent Cirelli could take her into protective custody.

Putting herself under Cirelli's protection wasn't the perfect solution, but maybe it was the best choice she had. She popped a square of emergency chocolate into her mouth—marshmallow-almond medley. She might have been good at running, but she couldn't count on being lucky forever. Asael was going to find her sooner or later. Murph had his own problems. It wasn't fair to draw him into hers.

She made the lasagna, stuck it into the oven, then began cleaning up. Murph shouldn't have to straighten up after her. She leaned into the fridge to drop some tomatoes she hadn't used back into the vegetable bin. She was straightening when a hand snaked around from behind her to seal her mouth.

"You get a point for being prepared," a faintly familiar voice whispered close to her ear as she struggled. Her gun was yanked from the back of her waistband and tossed into the living room, out of reach. "But lose a point for turning your back. You're not doing too well so far, Kate."

She was so stunned, she could barely mumble the single word against his palm. "Fred?"

"Call me Mordocai." Dark menace filled the man's words.

Murph had been right. Not Asael, after all.

Fear hit her hard, and she froze, couldn't think of a damn thing, not a single move Murph had shown her. *Fudge, fudge, fudge.*

"Stay quiet." Mordocai dragged her with him as he retreated, each step powerful and sure, no sign of his arthritic limp.

Then the adrenaline rush finally hit, and Kate tore at the hands that held her captive. "No!"

The single word she screamed against the man's fingers came through barely audible as he dragged her toward the back door.

"Where are you taking me?" she tried to ask, the sounds she was making nearly unintelligible.

He made out the words just fine.

"Somewhere private. We're going to have a little fun and a nice little chat. I have a couple of hours before my flight."

The broom leaned against the wall just ahead—close, closer, then finally close enough. She grabbed for the handle, but he thrust her forward at the same time, and she ended up knocking it over instead of grabbing it.

Okay, okay. What did Murph say?

Elbow to the stomach, head up, break the bastard's nose.

She steadied herself for a second, then did just as they'd practiced.

Mordocai's hands slipped on her. She dropped her full weight, grabbed the broom, jammed the handle into his groin. But as they struggled, the man shifted between her and the back door, so when she broke free at last, she had to run toward the front of the house.

What's next? What now?

Murph had put a gun in the kitchen drawer for her. Or…

Murph. He was out in the driveway. All she had to do was reach the front door.

She lunged. Failed. Mordocai plowed into her and knocked her face-first onto the hardwood floor at the bottom of the stairs.

Blood dripped from her nose as she struggled to turn to her back.

"Oh Kate." He was smiling at her as he fought her. "I do enjoy a tussle."

She caught a good look at him, for the first time. The

friendly mechanic she liked had been just an act and a lot of makeup. Mordocai wasn't nearly as old, more like Fred's younger, evil brother.

"Enjoy *this*," she gasped the words and brought her knee up as hard as she could. She caught him in the jaw, which made him swear and lose his grip on her long enough for her to slip out from under him. She scrambled forward, a mad race of limbs. Then she was on the stairs, leaping over three steps at a time, looking only where she was going, never turning back.

Upstairs bathroom. Lock the door. Done and done. Next, she tore the window open and shouted, "Murph!"

Except, Murph wasn't in the driveway. His shovel lay abandoned in a snow bank. Where the hell was he?

Had Mordocai killed him?

Kate's breath caught. *No, no, no.*

She searched for red on the snow, blood, while the door rattled and creaked as Mordocai threw his weight against it. She spun and watched the frame shake. Her heart slammed hard inside her chest in response to each bang.

She shrank into the farthest corner, grabbing the crowbar placed strategically under the sink, wishing she had a gun in there with her.

Bang!

The door was old, the wood dry, the top hinge loosening already. The pair of rusty screws tried to valiantly hold the line, do their duty, but they weren't going to make it. She had seconds.

She glanced at the window, then at the laundry chute. She went with the rabbit hole. "Here we go, Alice."

Down she slid, hugging the crowbar close to make sure it wouldn't catch, hoping she could get out of the house and reach the waiting Mustang Murph had left for her. She had to call the police for him. She couldn't bear thinking that something bad had happened to Murph.

In fact, as Kate thumped to the ground inside the laundry room, she refused to think about it. She tore the door open, but Mordocai was already there, waiting for her with a terrifying, cold smile on his almost-Fred face. She swung the crowbar, but he knocked her hand aside, then pinned her against the wall.

Then he grabbed her neck, and he squeezed and squeezed.

CHAPTER TWENTY

Murph stepped into his new neighbor's house in his socks. He'd left his boots in the garage, didn't want to give himself away by dragging mud inside.

He checked the large laundry room, his gaze drawn to the metal cabinet that stood as tall as he was, bolted to the wall. Gun cabinet? His gaze dropped to the heavy-duty lock. This could be where Wendy White kept the rifle he might or might not have seen from outside. Since he had no way of opening the lock, he walked into the kitchen. No guns in sight there, but he found plenty of large knives, stuck into a wooden block on the counter.

The furniture was sparse, low-end, the kind a person wouldn't mind leaving behind if they had to light out in a hurry. Everything was mismatched as if his new neighbor had furnished the house from the flea market that operated at the old county airport every Sunday. A picture on the wall caught Murph's eye, Wendy and two men, one who looked a few years older—boyfriend?—and a younger guy in his early twenties who could have been their son.

She seemed to be living here alone. Murph hadn't seen anyone but her around the house since he'd come home.

Kate hadn't mentioned anyone else either. So where was Wendy's family? Or maybe the family portrait was a fake, a decoy. Maybe she was a stone-cold assassin, and the Photoshopped picture and the frilly curtains were her cover.

Mindful of the time, Murph hurried to the small bedroom that held little more than a simple bed and an old dresser. *Bingo.* He grinned at a portable safe that sat on the bottom of the half-empty closet. He tried the lock, but opening it went beyond the powers of his pocketknife.

What was Wendy hiding in there? Information on Kate? More weapons? He pushed the safe aside but found nothing else save a plastic storage container filled with local maps.

As he straightened, he could hear the engine of a car outside, and he swore under his breath. Sounded like Wendy had decided to bring her lunch home today. Harper must have missed her.

Murph ran back to the laundry room, turned the lock and pulled the door closed behind him, jumped into his boots and cut through the garage, locked the door behind him there too, then waited, pressed against the siding. He didn't want Wendy catching him cutting across the strip of bushes between their yards.

The garage door rolled up, creaking. Okay, she wasn't walking to the front door. She was pulling the car in.

Murph inched up to look in through the window, squinted. *Wrong car.* The black BMW M5 was way out of place in his neighborhood.

He waited until the driver got out. As the man turned, preoccupied with his phone, Murph caught him in profile. He matched the younger man's photo on Wendy's family picture inside.

Murph ducked before he could be spotted, then ran toward his backyard, keeping down below window level. He darted through the bushes and kept in the cover of Wendy's shed until he reached the back of his own garage.

He went around, down the driveway, and picked up his

shovel, starting to work again, watching the neighbor's windows from the corner of his eye. He wanted to see if he could catch another glimpse of the guy, if he could figure out a way the man might be part of a planned hit. The physical exertion helped him think. The cold kept his head clear.

If Wendy was Asael's lover, the young guy could be Asael's son. Was the older guy on their family photo Asael?

Maybe murder was the family business. Maybe Wendy was ready to make her move on Kate and called in her son to help.

Okay, the theory was a stretch.

Assassins tended to be solitary. They didn't normally hunt in a family unit. Yet Interpol intelligence said Asael *had* pulled an odd job or two with his lover.

Murph swore under his breath, wishing he'd snapped a photo of that family picture with his cell phone so he could show it to Kate.

If Wendy was Asael's lover, then Asael could be tracked through her, and Kate would be free. As soon as the mystery guy left, Murph was heading next door again, this time with tools to open that gun cabinet and the safe. Hopefully, soon. The FBI was on their way to pick up Kate, and he had trouble processing the idea that he might never see her again. He might break down and beg her to stay and—.

A sharp series of beeps inside his house cut him off mid-thought. *Smoke detector.* Murph broke into a run. He banged on the door, even as he was reaching for his keys. "Kate!"

He unlocked the door, burst in, reached for the keypad to disable the security system, and found it already disabled. Everything snapped into sudden, cold focus.

Smoke poured out of the oven. He pulled his gun as he hurried to turn it off. "Kate?"

No response.

He ran down the hall to the bedroom. "Are you in

there?" He shoved the door open.

The room stood empty, her abandoned suitcase on the middle of the bed. Her Kevlar vest was hanging in the closet. She was gone.

* * *

Mordocai smiled as he drove in the gray winter afternoon. Dark clouds gathered in the sky. *Ominous.* He loved it when the weather matched his mood.

He'd have some playtime with Kate, then, before he boarded the plane to Montreal, he would mail her head in a cooler box to Hong Kong, to Asael.

The package would please Asael, but also establish Mordocai as a professional on the same level. He didn't like the current inequality in their relationship. Every once in a while, love required a larger-than-life gesture, something big, something memorable.

So the gift would be a theatrical gesture. So sue him. He'd grown up in the theater. Not on the stage, they'd said he wasn't handsome or talented enough for that. But he'd done makeup, created sets, dealt with everything that was mechanical, taught himself every aspect of the art, every backstage job. He would have done anything to stay near those red velvet curtains.

He'd met Asael in the theater—a young Adonis, with all that firm, sinuous flesh. Asael had been born to the stage—brilliant, full of defiance and anger and darkness. Violence shimmered oh so tantalizingly close to the surface—another layer of excitement. His presence filled the stage, seduced the audience. Mordocai became his admirer first, then his lover.

When a pissant administrator had tried to cause trouble for Asael, they went to his house and had a chat with him. His body had never been recovered.

Then Asael disappeared from Boston, and Mordocai had grieved for him for years. Until the prodigy popped up again, needing a complete transformation for a job. He had left the theater by then, found another line of work that satisfied his dark appetites more fully than fake blades and fake blood on the stage.

At first, Mordocai used his makeup talent to help. Then, eventually, Asael let him assist with bigger tasks. And now Mordocai would be the one to finish the witness bitch. He was out of the shadows at last. He was the main character, in the spotlight in the middle of the stage where he belonged.

He wanted his police sketch next to Asael's on the FBI's Most Wanted list. They were a couple. They should be together there.

Asael needed to understand that they were equals. In all the world, nobody measured up to him but Mordocai. Asael needed to understand that they belonged to each other, that his young fluff pieces on the side would no longer be tolerated.

Mordocai gripped the wheel. He would *not* be replaced in Asael's bed.

They were perfect for each other, alike in so many ways, although Asael preferred a quick job, while Mordocai liked to play if given the opportunity. He liked the rush of power.

He stepped on the gas and drove around a tractor trailer, careful not to swerve too sharply, mindful of Kate Bridges in the trunk. He preferred personally inflicting any banging up that happened to his victims.

CHAPTER TWENTY-ONE

Murph tore through the house, desperately searching for a clue that would tell him who'd taken Kate and where they'd gone.

The muddy footprints on the floor taunted him. The smattering of blood on the bottom stair was like a knife to his heart. She'd been hurt.

The busted bathroom door upstairs told a story. More signs of struggle in the laundry room, blood smears on the laundry chute as well.

Rage punched through him. Unproductive. He reached for the positive. *Not enough blood for the injury to be fatal.* He had every reason to believe that Kate had been alive when she'd been taken.

Alive but unarmed. He found her gun half under the couch in the living room. All his backup weapons were also still in their hiding places. Her phone and her purse were on the counter.

He needed a clue to follow, but no matter how carefully he looked, he found nothing inside the house, so he tried outside. Footprints in the snow out back led across the neighbor's yard and to the street. He ran as he followed them. The footprints led to tire tracks. Looked like, at one point, another car had parked behind the Mustang. Murph pulled his phone, then swore. The snow was too slushy to take a good picture of the tire marks for comparison with the tire tread database. No way for him to tell what kind of vehicle the bastard drove.

Frustration choked him, coupled with worry for Kate.

Had Wendy doubled back, come to his house while he'd been inside hers?

As he ran back home, he dialed Harper. "You got Wendy White?"

"Yeah. She's here at the station. Her car insurance expired. I can hold her until she fills out the paperwork and pays her fines, but not much longer. Want to tell me what this is about?"

"Not now." Murph hurried inside through the back, scanning every detail once again, looking for anything he might have missed earlier. "Patch me through to the captain."

As soon as Bing picked up, Murph said, "Kate's been kidnapped."

"When?"

"In the last hour. She was hiding in Broslin. She's the only person who's ever seen Rauch Asael and lived to tell the tale. Either he or someone connected to him came after her."

A second of stunned silence, then Bing snapped on the other end, "You couldn't tell me this before?" But he knew better than to waste time on being angry. "I'm putting out a statewide APB. You have a picture of her?"

"No."

"All right. I can give a fair description. You have any idea what kind of car we're looking for?"

"I wish. I shouldn't have let her out of my sight, dammit."

"Yeah," the Captain said in a grim tone, with feeling, as if he was thinking about his wife, Stacy. Then his voice turned into hard steel. "I'm sending everyone out on the roads. I'll call you back as soon as we have something."

Murph hung up so he could shrug into his harness. He shoved one handgun into that, another behind his back into his waistband. He swung his two rifles around his shoulder and grabbed the bag that held his extra bullets.

He was heading out when the doorbell rang. He tore the door open. And the next second, he was facing down three gun barrels.

"Drop your weapons!" Two men in black suits, a similarly dressed woman behind them—all trim, crisp and clean-cut, as if they'd just come off an assembly line—shouted all at once. "FBI. Drop your weapons!"

Jesus, not now. Murph slowly raised his hands in the air. No sudden movements. "Agent Cirelli and crew? I'm Murph Dolan. Kate has just been taken."

The woman—in her forties, permanent scowl, black hair shorter than Murph's military cut—stepped forward and disarmed him with a few efficient moves. "I want to see ID. Keep your hands up."

"Back pocket. On the right."

She reached for his wallet, flipped it open, checked. "Where's Miss Bridges?"

"I don't know. I was out shoveling snow. The kidnapper came in through the back door of the garage. He disabled the security system." Murph lowered his hands, ready to go. "We're wasting time."

"I talked to her earlier today." Cirelli said, while the other two spread through his house, all three keeping their weapons out. She eyed the reinforced door. "Kate asked me to come and get her."

"I wanted her safe." Murph snapped out the words.

"Clear," one of the male agents called from the bedroom.

The other one drummed down the stairs. "Upstairs too. But there's blood on the stairs. Consistent with a non-fatal injury."

Murph moved to push past Cirelli. "I don't have time for this. You stay and monkey around as long as you'd like."

Except, before he could take another step, he had the agent's Beretta right up against his chest. Cirelli had already lost Kate once. She appeared determined not to fail again.

"Everything will go easier if you cooperate, Mr. Dolan."

Then the other two were behind Murph, and the next second, he was in handcuffs, cold metal circling his wrists.

"Are you kidding me right now?" He gritted his teeth, everything inside him pushing him to fight. *To hell with cooperation. Head-butt Cirelli, shove the younger agent into the wall, then make a break for the door before the other one can react.*

But, dammit, cooperation probably *would* get him to Kate faster, so he held back, although it required every bit of self-control he had. *Play nice.*

"Hey, no need to be a hard-ass about this." Murph looked her in the eye. "I'm not the enemy here."

"Why don't I decide that?" Cirelli's face was set in a cold mask as she holstered her weapon. "How about the two of us go down to the local police station, where we can talk a little while the agents look through the house and figure out what happened?"

How long would that take? Murph's muscles bunched. He shook his head. "You're making a mistake."

They were wasting precious time, but resisting the agent would waste even more. Bing, Harper and Chase were out looking for Kate, but Leila would be at the station. She would vouch for Murph.

"Fine. Okay. Let's go." He strode through the door. "Every minute you're wasting on me, the kidnapper is getting farther away with her."

"Rauch Asael is still in Hong Kong," Cirelli said. "We're cooperating with the local authorities there on his apprehension. They found his lair this morning. Signs point to him being there just hours earlier."

"Kate was kidnapped by Asael's lover." He was never

going to forgive himself for not figuring that out sooner. "I have a handful of likely candidates." He swore as he hurried to the black SUV in his driveway with Cirelli on his tail.

The agent opened the back door for him. "Asael's long-term lover is an older man who calls himself Mordocai."

Murph's head spun as he slid onto the backseat. The word *older* reverberated in his brain. *Fred?* But Fred had checked out. Fred had been at the mechanic shop when the dark sedan had followed Kate.

Cirelli shoved behind the wheel, reaching for the GPS. She called the station, identifying herself as an FBI agent. She asked for assistance, an interview room, and a holding cell.

Murph could only shake his head in disgust in the back as she shot down the road. "If you want to catch Mordocai, you need to run a no-holds-barred FBI check on Fred Kazincky. You have access to data beyond the basic law enforcement databases."

The agent flashed him a skeptical look in the rearview mirror.

Anger pumped through Murph. He kept it in check. He needed cooperation, and blowing up on Cirelli wouldn't get him that. "What do you have to lose? I obviously don't have Kate. What if Kazincky does? I think he's Mordocai."

Cirelli hesitated for a moment but then called the name in, while Murph tried to think back to every single thing he knew about Fred.

"Around sixty," he told the agent. "New to town. Works as a mechanic at Arnie's Gas Station. Kate takes her car to him."

What else? *Nothing. Dammit.* Why hadn't he looked at Fred more closely?

He tried to remember any snippet of conversation with Kate that might have involved Fred, but couldn't remember anything significant. He racked his brain, even as Cirelli was pulling up to the station.

Bing waited for them outside. Leila must have called him back in. He blustered when the agent grabbed Murph from the back of the SUV.

"That's my officer." Bing strode toward them, eyes narrowed, shoulders squared. "I guarantee you're making a mistake here."

Cirelli escorted Murph past him. "Agent Cirelli, FBI. Your opinion will be taken into consideration, Captain."

Murph shot the man a placating look. Let Cirelli play the hotshot. He figured on ten minutes of interrogation, then they could finally focus on finding Kate. He could be patient for ten more minutes before murdering any FBI agents.

The station stood empty, save for Bing and Leila, everyone else out looking. Murph was grateful to Bing for that.

"I'm going to be present at the questioning, if you don't mind," Bing told Cirelli in a tone that made it clear he'd be there even if the agent did protest. He led them to the conference room instead of the interrogation room. "He doesn't need those cuffs."

"My case, my suspect." Cirelli pulled out a chair for Murph then walked to the opposite side of the table.

She didn't sit. She pinned Murph with a hard look. "How did you end up meeting Kate Bridges?"

"She snuck into my bed."

Bing shot Murph a don't-antagonize-her-look, while the agent raised a precise eyebrow.

Fine. Murph went ahead and explained the circumstances in as few words as possible.

"Why would she stay?" the agent asked.

"She had nowhere else to go. It's not like the FBI could protect her."

Bing shook his head.

"If she felt safe with you, why would she call me to get her out?"

"We had reason believe that Asael found her."

"You said it was Asael's lover." Cirelli braced her hands on the table. "Which one is it?"

"Mordocai. Took me a while to figure it out, all right?"

"What makes you think he's here?"

He told her, holding his boiling frustration in check, finishing with "That's all I know. Satisfied?" He pushed to his feet. "Now let me go so I can go and find her."

Instead of responding to him, the agent looked at Bing. "I'm going to need a holding cell, Captain."

Bing shoved his chair back. "Like hell. Everything he said is true. You're not going to lock up one of my officers."

"Are you refusing to assist the FBI?" Cirelli asked, her tone cool and hard. "Because I can have him put in a van and shipped to D.C."

Bing flashed her a look full of disgust. "I will be filing a complaint."

"You do that." Cirelli walked around to take Murph by the elbow. "It's temporary detainment. I need to keep Mr. Dolan secured until we thoroughly search his house and figure out what happened to Miss Bridges."

"Fred Kazincky took her!" Murph raised his voice for the first time. "Mordocai."

But the agent didn't listen, and he was in lockup by the time he realized he should have fought the feds right at the beginning, right before they'd slapped the cuffs on him. Which were left on, even if it was against regulation. Cirelli wouldn't listen to Bing about that either. She told Murph she'd be back shortly, then asked the captain to walk her out so she could ask him a few more questions.

Jerry, one of the town drunks, was the only other guest of the Broslin PD, in the smaller cell.

"Murph." The old geezer squinted against the neon lights overhead, coming up to his elbows on the bench where he'd been sleeping. "Never thought we'd be neighbors back here."

Murph grunted in response, pacing his cell that smelled like disinfectant, his thoughts turning darker and darker.

Kate had been living in his house. She'd called for help to get out. The feds caught him with a bunch of weapons, ready to run. *Fresh from the war. Injured. Probably unhinged.* That was what they would think.

Before long, they'd convince themselves that he'd killed her. Then they'd start looking for the body. They wouldn't find it. Maybe they'd bring in equipment to dig around out back. Freaking *hours* could pass before they came back to interrogate him again.

Murph kicked the bars, startling Jerry awake again.

"Easy now," the old man mumbled. "Some of us are tryin' to catch some shuteye 'round here."

Murph ignored him. *Think!* What did he know for sure? Mordocai hadn't killed Kate on sight. He'd taken her, which meant the bastard wanted more than a quick kill. Murph couldn't bear thinking about what that might be. He had to get the hell out of here. Mordocai wouldn't play with her forever. They were running out of time.

Murph was ready to tear the cell apart with his bare hands by the time Bing hurried back, his jaw set tight.

"How in hell did you get yourself into this mess? The FBI wouldn't tell—"

"You have to let me go." Murph stepped up to the door. "If I don't find her, she's dead."

"We're looking. I'm heading back out."

"I can't sit here while she's being tortured or worse. I'm asking you as a friend. They're not going to find her body at my house. I swear."

"If you think you have to tell me that—" Bing's expression darkened. His hand came up in a frustrated gesture. "They might try to pin this on you without the body."

"Not if I bring her back."

Bing dropped his hand. "You just trust the law and stay put. I hear you were back here the other night. Lock got beat up. That's government property. You better calm down if you want your badge back. I'm telling you this as a friend,

Murph. You have your job waiting for you when your shoulder heals. Harper's been using your cruiser while his was in the shop, but he just returned the keys to my desk this morning. Anyway, I'm heading out to look for Kate."

He moved over to the next cell and unlocked it. "I'm letting you go, Jerry. I don't have time to worry about you today. You go straight home and sober up, all right? Don't get into any more trouble."

Jerry, knowing a good deal when he heard one, slid off the bench hurried forward. "Yes, sir, Captain."

Murph looked after them as they left, both in a hurry, neither man looking back. Relief washed over him. Bing's message had been loud and clear. The lock on Murph's cell was broken, the keys to his old cruiser were on the captain's desk, and everybody was heading out, the station empty.

He sat down on the ground, looped his arms over his feet and brought his handcuffed hands from his back to the front. He waited another minute to make sure Bing and Jerry were out of the building, then he lifted the door and rattled it. That didn't do the trick. But when he dropped the door back down and leaned forward to check it out, he could see that Bing was right. The locking mechanism was definitely damaged enough so it would have to be replaced if they wanted to keep the criminals inside the cell.

He fisted his hands and smashed the lock with the base of his wrists, using the handcuffs to attack metal with metal. It didn't work. All he accomplished was bending the handcuffs a little and scraping off some skin.

He discarded his next idea outright: ramming the door—a bad idea with his injuries. Instead, he backed up a step and executed a textbook roundhouse kick. Then another and another. Then he lifted and rattled the door again, and the next second he was free.

He hurried up front and popped his head out of the hallway carefully.

Nobody in the office. He didn't stop to wonder where Leila had conveniently disappeared. *Thank you, Captain.*

He ran to Bing's desk, looked for a handcuff key first, found one pretty easily—almost as if left out on purpose—but when he turned it in the lock, only one side popped open. He tried it again. Nothing. He banged it against the edge of the desk in vain, accomplishing nothing but skinning his wrist again. He was too frantic with worry for Kate to feel pain.

He left the open cuff dangling, yanked the top desk drawer out and found the cellphone Cirelli had taken off him. It sat right next to his wallet and Bing's backup weapon. He grabbed all three, then the keys to his old cruiser. Having the police radio would be an advantage. He could keep up with what law enforcement was doing.

He snuck out the back and drove to Arnie's. The cruiser cut through traffic, people moving out of his way. He was there in five minutes.

No sign of Fred, not that Murph had expected to see him there. He parked in the front and hurried in. *Hang in there, Kate. Just hang in there. I'm coming.*

Arnold Martin had been one of Murph's father's drinking buddies back in the day. Except Arnie had given up the bottle, settled down and built a decent life for himself. Now he had more fat rolls than teeth, but his wife, Juliana, loved him anyway.

Murph found the guy in his cramped, windowless office in the back, bleak as shit but he hadn't come to sightsee. "I need everything you have on Fred Kazincky."

"Murph." The man nodded in greeting, snapping his bushy gray eyebrows together. "What's this about now?"

"I need Fred's employment file. Everything you have on him."

"He didn't come in this morning. I can't give you his file. Are you all right? What's with the handcuffs?"

"Misunderstanding with the FBI. The bastard took Kate."

"Who?"

"Fred kidnapped Kate Concord. The new waitress at

the diner. I don't think she has much time left."

"That sweet girl who brings her Chevy here?" Arnie stared, confusion in his eyes. "Are you sure? Why on earth would Fred do that?"

"He's a professional hit man. Kate's been hiding in town. He's been after her all along."

Those bushy eyebrows slid way up, then Arnie blinked a couple of times as he tried to process the information. "Like witness protection?"

"The whole police station is out looking for her. Even the FBI is here. She's running out of time."

Murph was ready to go through the man and apologize later, but Arnie made his decision and heaved off of his chair, yanked his keys from his pocket and hurried to the file cabinet, at last, unlocked it and produced Fred Kazincky's manila folder.

Murph took it with a nod. "I appreciate it. You know what he drives?"

"A beat-up black Dodge pickup. But it's in front of his apartment. I saw it when I went out for coffee. Anyway, he wouldn't get far in that." Arnie scowled as he paused. Then his eyes narrowed. "A red Mazda 6 was stolen overnight from the service bay. I reported it to Bing first thing this morning." He rifled through the papers on his desk and pushed one toward Murph, tapped it with his finger. "That's the license plate number."

Murph stored it in his brain. "Did you ever see him drive a dark blue sedan? Maybe something you guys use as a loaner?"

"Nah. We don't have loaners. We ain't that fancy."

"If there's anything else you can think of about Fred that might help…"

Arnie just scratched his chin, looking stunned and bewildered, so Murph thanked him then moved on. As soon as he was in the cruiser, he let Bing know that they were likely looking for the red Mazda Arnie had already reported. He left it to the captain to update the FBI, and moved on to combing through Fred's employment file.

He found nothing useful there, except Fred's address, a second-floor apartment in a run-down apartment complex.

Murph drove there next. Ten more minutes. *Dammit.*

A familiar trio of scruffy teens loitered by the door, Robbie and his buddies.

Murph fixed them with a look as hard as he could make it. "You've seen Fred Kazincky today?"

Shrugs all around.

Then the youngest kid said, without meeting Murph's eyes. "Not today, man."

While Robbie glared, asking with a sneer, "What the old guy do? Didn't pay a parking ticket?"

Murph hurried past the snickering teens, up the stairs. Mordocai wouldn't have brought Kate back here, but he might have been careless enough to leave a clue behind. He wasn't Asael. He was just a sidekick. Faint hope, but it was the only hope Murph had, so he clung to it.

The apartment was at the end of a dank hallway, the door open to a crack. Murph pushed his way in with his gun drawn, but the place was empty, completely stripped, as if nobody had ever lived there.

No clues. Not as much as a crumpled take-out receipt in the garbage. *Nothing.*

The linoleum floor had been vacuumed and mopped, the faint scent of bleach in the air. Mordocai might have been just a sidekick, but he knew what he was doing.

Murph called Bing again and gave him the address.

"Want me to head over there?" the Captain asked.

"No hurry," Murph told him. "Keep looking for Kate. I doubt you'll find as much as a fingerprint here."

CHAPTER TWENTY-TWO

As pain sliced through Kate's shoulder, she shifted, petrified, half-frozen, but not yet beaten. Hope kept her going as she shivered in the cold. Thank God, she'd put on her ugly Christmas sweater.

In the past two years, this was her second time locked in a trunk. Except, the first time, the car had been carrying her to life; while this time, it was speeding her to death.

The ropes that bound her cut off circulation in her hands, which made it difficult to fish around for her phone in her back pocket, the cheap disposable she'd used to call Cirelli.

She could reach the top, her fingers touching the plastic, but the phone kept slipping from between her fingertips when she tried to pull it out. Then, breathing hard from the effort, every muscle clenched, she finally managed. The phone came out halfway, then all the way at last.

Don't drop it, don't drop it, don't drop it. Of course, she did. The stupid thing slipped from her frozen fingers.

Long minutes passed before she found it, before she brought the phone to the front, praying the car wouldn't stop and Mordocai wouldn't come for her yet.

She dialed Murph. The call rang out just as the car turned, slowed, then came to a halt.

"Pick up. Please, pick up," she whispered into the darkness, knowing he might not, since he had no way of knowing she was the caller. Her name wouldn't come up on his display. He might take her for spam.

The car rocked as Mordocai got out from behind the steering wheel. His car door slammed.

Kate expected the trunk to pop open any second, for her reprieve to be over. She held her breath, but the boots crunching snow kept going. She could hear other cars, then a familiar click somewhere behind her head, like the gas tank cover popping open. A metallic, scraping sound came next. The nozzle inserted?

Then the line was picked up at last. "Murph Dolan."

His sure, strong voice spread hope through her and gave her something to hang on to. His presence filled the trunk, and suddenly she wasn't alone.

"It's me," she whispered, tears burning her eyes. "I'm in the trunk. It's Fred."

"I know. Where are you? Are you all right?"

"I'm at a gas station."

"Does the trunk have a safety release? It should be up in the middle, glowing in the dark."

"I tried it already. It's disabled."

"Any tools? See if you can find a tire iron. You might be able to bust the lock open."

Right. She pinched the phone between her shoulder and her ear to free her hands. She'd done a cursory search already, before deciding that going for the phone was her best chance. But now she stretched farther, moved around until she reached every corner. If she found the tire iron, at least she'd have a weapon when Mordocai came for her.

Her cold fingers probed every nook. She touched nothing but carpeting. Desperation washed through her. "There's nothing."

"I'm coming to get you." His voice was tight. "Don't

you give up for a second." A growl of frustration came through the line, then, "Okay. Look for a little knob, up in the back in the corners somewhere, attached to a wire. There should be one on each side."

Oh God, the buttons that released the backseat to fold down. Why hadn't she thought of that? Probably because her mind was frozen with fear.

For long moments, her frantically seeking fingers found nothing, and she panicked, thinking Mordocai had cut off the buttons. But then she found the wire and followed along, reached the end, and the button was still attached. She pushed as hard as she could and leaned against the back of the seat. When it finally budged, tears sprung into her eyes.

"I got it."

She pushed an inch at a time, until she could see out. Mordocai stood up front, cleaning the windshield. She only saw his arm, sweeping back and forth. Then the pump clicked, the tank full, and she held her breath while he walked around to take care of that.

"What do you see?" Murph's voice dripped with tension.

"Hang on." She craned her neck. "A highway sign. PA Turnpike Northeast Extension."

"Do you see the name of a town?"

"No." And she didn't dare push the seat farther down for fear that Mordocai might notice. She'd risked enough already. She pulled back and eased the seat back into place, then dropped onto her side while gasping for air.

"Kate?"

She scrambled to think. "Hang on."

Okay, what did she have? She couldn't make a run for it. She was tied up. Mordocai would see her the second she pushed that seat all the way down. She would never make it out of the car. Yelling for help was futile. He was the closest; he would get to her first. He had a gun with a silencer.

She could hear him walking around the car, opening

the driver's side door. She swallowed her panic. There was still hope. As long as they hadn't reached their final destination, she was still okay.

"We're leaving. I need to hang up. The battery is getting low." She wanted to save some juice for later, just in case. "Look for a red Mazda."

"Hang in there. I'm coming." Plenty of worry and frustration tinged Murph's voice, but she knew that he meant every word, and that he'd die before he broke his promise.

"I know," she said, and then she disconnected.

* * *

Murph flew down the road with the siren blaring, grateful to Bing for the cruiser. He had no idea how much of a time advantage Mordocai had.

The bastard could have left the second he'd snatched Kate, or he could have hung around a while to watch Murph go nuts, watch the FBI arrive. Maybe he got off on that kind of thing.

He dialed Bing's number once again. "It's definitely Fred. He's traveling on the PA Turnpike Northeast Extension. Going west." Since the Northeast Extension started at Plymouth Meeting, about thirty miles from Broslin, west was the only way the man could have taken. "Driver is armed and dangerous. Kidnap victim confirmed in trunk. Exercise maximum caution."

He ended the call and focused on the road as he flew down Rt. 476, then onto the Northeast Extension. He knew the car he was looking for, and he would recognize Mordocai. His mind was razor sharp, focused.

Passing the physical, getting back on the force, finishing his house—none of that mattered now, only finding Kate. He could give up everything else, just as long as he got her back.

Two state troopers zoomed by. Good. Bing had put out the APB. Murph wondered if the FBI was still wasting their time at his house. He couldn't worry about them now.

All he could think of was Kate.

His phone rang. Unidentified number. Same as before.

"We're off the highway," Kate whispered as soon as he picked up, her voice sending a spiral of relief through him. "On a dirt road. He just stopped."

"How many turns did he take? How many times did he slow?"

"Just straight to the dirt road," she said, and then the line went dead.

What exit? What dirt road? Highways didn't intersect with dirt roads for the most part. They connected to off-ramps and other major thoroughfares.

Except for the pull-offs cops use to catch speeders.

Some officers liked to hide behind signs; others parked behind bushes with their radar guns. They all had their favorite spots.

Murph kept his eyes open for a place like that, somewhere that would be concealed from oncoming traffic but would have visibility over a long stretch of highway the opposite way. Since he knew exactly the kind of prime speed-trap spot he was looking for, he found it in less than twenty minutes.

Fresh tire marks in the snow.

Bingo.

He shut off his siren and pulled off the road, stopped the car. He could see something red among the bushes fifty feet ahead on an incline. He nosed the cruiser forward a foot at a time until he could finally see into the other vehicle.

Empty. Nobody in sight. But the yew bushes behind the Mazda spread wide enough to hide several people.

He called in his position, then slipped out, took cover, pointed his gun at those bushes. "Police. Come out with your hands in the air!"

No response, no movement. He inched forward, ready for anything as he rounded the Mazda, noting the trampled snow. The trunk stood open by a small gap. He held his breath as he opened it all the way, praying he wouldn't find a body.

Then he drew a ragged breath. Kate wasn't in there. No blood on the carpet.

Thank you, God. Please don't let me be late.

He skirted the bushes next but found nothing behind them, so he scanned the open fields ahead. A line of footprints led that way, to the edge of the woods. Did Mordocai have another car waiting somewhere up ahead on a little country road?

Murph hoped against hope that wasn't the case. He hoped Mordocai had simply gotten spooked by all the police on the highway and pulled off.

A water tower glinted in the winter sunshine above the tree line. That meant a town. Murph broke into a run. He had to catch up with them before Mordocai could steal a car and disappear with Kate.

He reached the woods, gasping icy air. He was out of shape. What little workout he'd been getting at the station these last couple of days was nothing. He'd been out of the action for too long because of his injuries. But he couldn't fail Kate.

He followed the tracks in the snow for a good twenty minutes before he caught a glimpse of purple. Her ridiculous Christmas sweater? He pushed forward.

The purple wasn't moving. After a dozen or so careful steps, he realized why. She was tied to a tree, her head hanging, her auburn hair disheveled and loose from her ponytail, obscuring her features.

So help me God, if the bastard hurt her— Murph's heart raced. *Move. Be alive.*

Then she looked up, a piece of cloth hanging from her mouth, a gag.

A moment of pure relief came first, before the cold fury that coursed through Murph as he slipped behind an oak tree. *Careful now.* If she was out here like that, alive, it could mean only one thing: Mordocai had seen him and set a trap.

As if to confirm his suspicion, a voice rang out. "I'm glad you could join us. You caused me so much trouble, I hated leaving you behind, Officer Dolan."

Murph could identify the man's location by the sound, but didn't look that way. Doing what assassins did might have been Mordocai's expertise, but Murph wasn't a novice in the game of search and destroy either. He knew the rules of engagement.

He inched forward, pulling behind some evergreens for cover. Mordocai could blanket the position with bullets, but he wouldn't know where exactly his target was or if it'd been hit.

The spot was great while Murph measured up the situation and gained his bearings, but he couldn't stay there until reinforcements arrived. He had to move forward and get Mordocai in his sights. He had to protect Kate, who was out in the open.

A dark, violent movie played in the back of his mind, his team leaving cover and being ripped to shreds, explosions shaking the ground, blood everywhere. A bolt of pain shot through his shoulder, and he couldn't move. *Hold position.* The order he should have given.

He could smell the smoke and the sulfur and the blood. He could hear the screams.

Hold position.

His body felt paralyzed. Cold sweat beaded on his forehead.

But then he thought of Kate's sparkling blue eyes, wrestled the past aside and shrugged out of his coat, hung it on a branch so Mordocai could see patches of the fabric through the gaps between branches.

Murph carefully dropped to his stomach and crawled forward. A fallen tree provided him with cover for the first twenty feet. He ignored the gruesome memories that tried to push into his mind. He ignored the cold too, as bad as in the Afghan mountains in winter during his first deployment.

Search and destroy. He looked forward to getting to the

second part.

He left the cover of the log and crawled behind a scraggly bush that didn't have a single dried-up leaf left on the branches, not much to hide him. He moved. Stopped. Moved again. No shots rang out. Mordocai was probably still watching his coat.

"I could hit you any time," the idiot bragged, his voice amplified, carrying a theatrical tone. "But I'm going to make you watch me put a bullet into her heart first. I don't like it when secondary characters disrupt my plans. And you're not even that. You're just a walk-on, you know that? The nameless guy who gets killed in the third act. I'm an assassin."

Murph moved into position, scanned the spot where the voice was coming from and saw a small movement halfway up a tree. Mordocai had gone for high ground. Smart. Smarter still would have been to keep his mouth shut.

Murph had the bastard's hiding place. Half the battle won. Only half. Mordocai perched behind an evergreen, the branches obscuring him as he kept shifting. No way to hit him.

Behind him, the round receptacle of the water tower peeked through a narrow gap between trees, clearly visible in the distance, right at the same level as Mordocai's head.

So Murph aimed for the tower, then moved the crosshairs to the left by a fraction of an inch, the handcuffs still dangling from his wrist.

"I'm an assassin!" Mordocai shouted with the overdone drama of a bad stage actor, sure of himself.

Murph took his shot and dropped the bastard right out of the tree.

Then he stood. "I'm an American soldier, you son of a bitch."

Sirens wailed in the distance as he ran forward to make sure Mordocai was dead. He kept his gun out until he reached the body that lay at an unnatural angle in a spreading pool of blood. "He's down and out!"

The assassin's eyes stared frozen at the sky, disbelief etched on his face. He was not getting up again—now or ever. Murph kicked the man's weapon away, out of habit, before he ran to Kate.

"Are you all right?" He pulled the rag from her mouth, and as she gasped for air, he filled his own lungs. He hadn't drawn a full breath since he'd found her gone. For a moment, the long moment it took for his heart to restart, he rested his forehead against hers. "I've got you," he whispered as he pulled back.

Her hair a messy jumble around her face, she kept smiling at him through her tears. "I knew you would come. I fought him every step of the way. I wanted to give you time to get here."

Murph's chest swelled with pride. "That's my girl." She was brave, tough, and so beautiful she made his heart ache. "Are you hurt anywhere?"

If the bastard had touched her, Murph was going to shoot him again.

Her lips stretched into a tremulous smile. "I'll take bruised and alive over the alternative."

Yeah. So would he. As he cut her ropes, his left arm began to shake. He hadn't even felt his injury until this moment. And now he didn't care. She was alive. Nothing else mattered.

Then she was free at last, and he gathered her against him. Her arms went around his neck, her face pressed against the crook of his shoulder. They held each other tightly, silently, appreciating that they had each other. He inhaled her scent—chocolate, what else—luxuriating in the feeling of having her in his arms. He never wanted to let her go. He couldn't bear thinking about how differently this all could have ended.

Way too soon, she pulled back, her gaze searching his. "Thank you."

"You can make me another lasagna. The first one

burned," he said, and then he kissed her.

A man could get obsessed with a mouth like hers. Her soft lips fit perfectly against his. He nudged, nibbled, licked, tasted. He ran his tongue along the seam of her lips. Then he swept inside and made her mouth his.

She didn't play coy. She gave as good as she got. Another thing he admired about her. He could have kept on kissing her forever.

Heat and need filled him, kicked up a notch when a soft, sexy moan escaped her throat. An urgency to take her and make her his pushed all other thought from his head. He wanted his mouth on every inch of her body, and hers on every inch of his—right then and there, against the tree.

He nudged her back, covered her body with his, slid a hand under her purple sweater, under her shirt, until his fingertips touched skin.

He was as hard as gunmetal. But before he could have lost it completely, the state police appeared, running out of the trees with guns drawn, shouting for hands in the air. *Oh hell.* And then, of course, a minute later, the FBI arrived, to make Murph's day complete.

Agent Cirelli and her team weren't amused by the jailbreak.

Cirelli pulled a fresh set of handcuffs from her belt. "I'm going to have to take you back into custody."

"He saved me!" Kate tried to step between them, but Murph offered his banged-up wrists.

He could explain himself to the agents later. Kate was chilled through. His priority was to get back to the station where she'd be warm and safe.

CHAPTER TWENTY-THREE

Kate was coming out of Murph's bathroom, finally clean and wearing dry clothes, when Cirelli walked into the bedroom, looking annoyed.

"Murph Dolan has been protecting me all this time," Kate told her again.

"He's a free man. But he should not have interfered. If he hadn't shot Mordocai, we could be interrogating the man right now. He might have given up Asael for a reduced sentence." Cirelli nodded toward Kate's suitcase. "Are you done packing?"

"Almost." Kate hesitated. "I feel safe here."

"Asael is still out there. You're safest with the US Marshals service, in the witness protection program. I've made contact. They're expecting you."

Her voice was clipped, her tone cold. She *was* seriously pissed. She had not liked Murph's interference, nor Kate's year-and-a-half-long disappearing act. She clearly resented that Kate hadn't trusted her enough to check in and let her know that she was alive all this time. When the setup at the funeral had gone wrong, Cirelli had lost both Asael *and* Kate. *Did that hurt her record?* The thought had never occurred to Kate before—she'd been too busy running—but now that it did, she flinched.

"Thank you. Thank you for everything," she said, then fell into an exhausted, awkward silence.

The adrenaline rush of the rescue over, she felt as if the very marrow had been drained out of her bones. Or as if something vitally important had been drained out of her. Her heart ached at the thought of leaving. "I wish I didn't have to go."

Every place she'd lived, she'd been super careful not to make close friends, not to put down roots, not to fall in love.

She wasn't sure she even believed in falling in love, let alone this fast. She wasn't big on trust. And now, here she was, on the brink of crying, because her heart was lost. God, how could she have been this stupid?

"Hey," Murph appeared in the doorway, shooting Cirelli as cold a look as the agent was shooting him.

As he walked in, Cirelli walked out, neither saying a word to the other in passing.

He stepped to the bed and began folding up Kate's patchwork quilt, not looking the least torn about her imminent departure. That hurt too, more than she'd thought was possible.

"The Witness Security Program we have in this country is top of the line," he said with full cop confidence, the reasonable voice of the law. "They'll keep you safe. They've never lost a single person who followed the instructions and was protected by the marshals. Not one. It's not like in the movies where the bad guys come and shoot up safe houses left and right. The marshals know what they're doing."

"Trusting the system doesn't come easy for me."

"I know. But you'll be safe. I promise."

Maybe, deep down, he loved her and only let her go for her own good. Maybe he was crying inside but was just one of those guys who couldn't show his feelings.

She gave a mental eye roll. Or maybe she was one of

those delusional women who believed what they wanted to believe, pretending some great romance where none existed.

"You've moved before." He stepped toward her. "You kept yourself safe. This is the same, except with a little extra help. This time, you'll be even safer."

Her throat burned. For the first time, she wanted more than just to be safe. She wanted to be loved.

"I liked being on the move, because I could control it. I don't like other people to have power over me, even if it's the US Marshals Service."

"You can make a new home."

"I want my old home back," she said on reflex. Then she paused. Did she?

Yes, she wanted her parents and Emma to be in her life again, but was she going to go back to live in LA? She desperately wanted a home, but maybe it was time for her to make a home of her own somewhere else. She could do that. She could actually put down roots if she stopped running and settled down somewhere.

"I could make a home in Broslin." She could see herself living here long-term.

Murph shook his head as he watched her, his expression unreadable. "Asael is still alive. You're no longer just a witness who got away, but also the woman who caused the death of his lover. That's the way he'll see it, even if you weren't the one to pull the trigger."

"Fudge him," she said with feeling. She was sick and tired of Asael in her life. But then the next thought froze her in place. The air got stuck in her lungs. "*You* took out Mordocai. Asael could come after *you*."

A scary, cold grin spread on his face. "If I could be sure of that, I'd sit tight right here and wait for him. Believe me, I'd love for things to go down that way."

"I want to stay too." Not that he'd asked her. Okay, obviously, she had no pride. But she felt safe here with Murph. They had the house fortified. They had defeated Mordocai. Murph could get treatment, recover. Maybe they could defeat Asael too, together, if he ever came.

Murph brought the quilt over and dropped it into her suitcase. He held her gaze, standing a hairsbreadth from her. He had an incredible presence, energy that irresistibly drew her. She swayed forward.

Slowly, watching her, he reached up and cupped her face. His fingers were warm and gentle on her skin. His mouth, the cold smile long gone, hovered just inches from hers. She could have wept with need.

The good-bye kiss, she thought. She wished they could have more, but since this was all she could get, she was going to take it. She was going to carry the memory of it when she went, and she—

He dipped his head and brushed his lips over hers.

Her knees trembled. She wanted the moment to last forever. She wanted him. She dropped the sweater she was folding and linked her arms around his waist as she snuggled against the hard planes of his chest.

When he would have stepped back—there were two FBI agents in the kitchen—she held on and kept on kissing him. He gave a fierce growl, like a tiger catching up to his dinner. The kiss changed tone, grew more heated, then, within a second, more desperate.

She slipped a hand under his shirt. The warm muscles in his lower back shifted as he gathered her even closer, and she caressed them with her seeking fingers, kneading her way up his back.

A ragged groan escaped his throat. "There'll be time for this later."

After Asael had been caught? He meant, when she was safe, she could come back. But who knew how long that would take? Her boobs could be hanging to her belly button by that stage. She wanted him *now*.

She fitted her lips back against Murph's, and they got lost in each other again, as one minute grew into another.

"If we're going to stop, we better stop now," he warned again in a tortured whisper against her lips.

She didn't think she could walk away from him. She didn't want to. He'd started out as an unexpected complication in her life, but in just a short time, he'd become important to her. "Don't stop."

His dark-chocolate eyes narrowed. He picked her up and strode into the bathroom with her, then locked the door behind them.

She was shrugging out of her clothes even as the lock clicked. While she stepped out of her shoes and pants, he undressed himself with military speed, then stood in front of her naked.

Wowee. Okay, then. He was giving her the full military salute and then some. The fact that he wanted her just as much as she wanted him was extremely gratifying. When he moved closer, her breath hitched.

Heat and raw sexual energy filled the air between them. Crackling.

His scars didn't detract from the beauty of his magnificent, battle-honed body, muscles everywhere, primal masculine energy radiating off him. She reached back for the clasp of her bra, but he turned her and took care of it, going to his knees before he drew her panties down, tossing them aside. He kissed his way up her legs, then as he stood, her back. Her body grew wet for him.

From the corner of her eye she could see as he reached for his bathroom box he'd brought up from the basement and pulled out a foil wrapper. He took care of protection, then turned her around to taste her lips once again. He kissed her with reverence, with so much gentleness that her heart melted.

"I wanted our first time to be slow. I wanted us to be able to take our time with each other," he whispered against her temple, his voice strangled as if somehow he considered it a personal failure that they'd ended up here like this, without any significant horizontal surface, wedged between the shower and the sink.

She couldn't respond, and he didn't wait for words. He

dipped his head to the sensitive skin of her neck below her ear, and he tasted her there, his hot tongue gliding along her skin.

He made her head spin even before he reached his hands under her thighs to lift her up and onto him, turning to back her against the door, the largest free space. He filled her completely, stretched her to the limit, suffused her with pleasure. She wrapped her legs around his waist and held on for the ride.

He was inside her so deeply they weren't even separate entities anymore; they were welded together.

"There are FBI agents waiting for us in the kitchen." She found the faint voice of reason, way too late.

A wry smile twisted his lips. "I've been deployed for the last eight months, then titillated by you for days on end. It'll only take two seconds."

Laughter bubbled up her throat. "Words every woman wants to hear."

Then he began to move, and she forgot all about the agents. She wound her arms around his neck. "You think I'm titillating?"

"Every moment of every day."

He supported her weight with his good arm, which gave his left hand a chance to cup her breast. His thumb played a torturous game with her nipple while his tongue conquered her mouth. His steady, deep strokes sent her body higher and higher. She could barely hear the door rattling with every thrust. She didn't care. *Sweet cocoa-bean heaven.*

They didn't have much time, but she didn't need much. Her world exploded when he squeezed her nipple and shifted her at the same time to fill her more fully yet.

She clung to him as pleasure shook her. They clung to each other.

She thought she'd been drained when they'd returned home from the police station after giving their statements, but now she was truly and completely depleted.

"This is ridiculous," she said as they dressed a minute later, her knees weak, her mind still lost in a fog of pleasure. "They can't make me go if I don't want to."

"You're going."

Disappointment burst her bubble of bliss. "You don't want me here."

"I want you safe."

"I'm safe with you." She opened the door and stepped out into the bedroom, looking back at him. She simply stated the fact. She wasn't going to beg. If he didn't want her, she was at least going to leave with some dignity. She could cry her eyes out later.

Murph followed her. "Damn right, I can keep you safe. That's why I'm coming with you." His eyebrows slid up. "Unless you have any objections?"

His words slammed into her and left her breathless. "You'd leave Broslin?"

He looked at her as if she was nuts. "Did you think I was just going to wave you good-bye and let you walk away alone? What the hell, Kate?"

She didn't respond. She didn't know what to think anymore.

He shook his head. "I figured out something while I was hurtling down the highway at a hundred miles an hour, trying to catch up to you. I'd be way more miserable without you than without Broslin." He stepped toward her. "The way I see it, I can have another surgery. I can heal. Maybe I could be a cop again here. But maybe that's not what I need. I've seen enough murder and violence. This could be my chance to open a new chapter. I need to figure out what that chapter is, and I want to figure it out with you. You seem to be good at moving on and surviving. How about giving me some tips?"

To hell with decorum. Kate threw herself into his arms. And then she did her best to kiss the self-satisfied smirk off his face.

Until someone cleared his throat behind her.

The agents were standing in the doorway. All three of them. Watching with undisguised interest.

Oh God. How long had they been there?

CHAPTER TWENTY-FOUR

Murph watched a blush spread on Kate's face, and he turned to glare at the agents. He'd about had it with them in his house.

Agent Cirelli cleared her throat. "I owe you an apology, Mr. Dolan."

He wondered who she'd talked to while he'd been in the bathroom with Kate. His commanding officer at the Reserves?

He rubbed his wrist that the broken cuff had scraped bloody. "You were doing your job. Apology accepted." Kate was here safe and sound; he could afford to be magnanimous. His body was sated and humming with contentment. That helped.

"Hey." Bing came up behind the agents and pushed inside. "Thought I'd stop by to make sure everything's going okay here."

"Thanks."

Bing looked Kate over first, then Murph, as the agents backed away. "You two okay?"

Murph rubbed his wrist again as the weirdest thought popped into his mind, a snippet of a memory. *Wait. No.*

Could it? "Robin Combs."

Bing raised his eyebrows. "What about her? She lose your mail?"

"She had a dream that I was shooting at a water tower while handcuffed."

"What water tower?"

"Never mind." But then something else occurred to him, and he called out to the agents, "Would one of you go out and see if there's a thresher in my barn?"

"A what?" one of them asked.

"Big piece of farm equipment," Bing explained.

The agents looked at him as if he'd gone crazy, so Murph turned back to Kate. "You keep packing. I'm going to step out for a minute."

Bing went with him. "What's this about?"

"I can't explain. A feeling. Let's just see." He hurried back and knew he hit pay dirt when he saw that the padlock wasn't the one he'd snapped on last year. "Mind shooting that off?"

"You get stranger and stranger. You know that?" Bing shook his head. "Forget it. I'm not even going to ask why." He pulled his Swiss Army knife and removed the screws that held the bracket. "By the way, you're not on the battlefield anymore. We don't shoot guns in people's back yards, if it can be helped."

They pushed the heavy door aside together. Then they stared at the threshing machine inside. Big, yellow, top of the line. *What the hell?*

Murph filled his lungs with cold night air. "Anyone reported one of these stolen?"

Bing rubbed the back of his neck. "No. But there'd be no reason a farmer would be checking on his thresher in the middle of winter. Whoever it belongs to might not have noticed yet that it's missing."

That sounded reasonable. "Are you thinking what I'm thinking?"

"The Tractor Trio likes to drive large farm equipment

through the front windows of banks." Bing's eyes narrowed. "How did it get here?"

Murph backed out and looked around. "I've been out a lot, going around, taking care of business. Kate works a regular shift. It wouldn't have been hard to find time when neither of us was around. We had plenty of snow lately. I never saw any tracks, but they would have been covered in ten or twenty minutes."

One of the FBI boys loped around the corner of the house to see what they were doing.

Bing waved him back. "Stay right there. This here might be an unrelated crime scene. I don't want any extra footprints."

Murph scanned the landscaping, considering all the possibilities. The thresher couldn't have come up his driveway—his woodpile was in the way—but it could have rolled over through any of his neighbors' treeless yards.

In a split second, everything fell into place.

"Wendy White. Moved next door recently. Has a boyfriend and a grown son. According to Kate, neither live with her. So that they're not seen together? I've been over to her house and happened to see a serious gun cabinet and a safe. Her son drives a black BMW M5."

"V-10 engine, 500 horsepower," Bing said. "Tops out at 155 miles per hour."

"Getaway car."

Bing looked toward the neighbor's house with interest. "Still not exactly a smoking gun."

"She eats at the Main Street Diner three times a day."

Bing's expression turned speculative. "Sitting at a table where she can have the bank across the road in sight?"

"I'd be willing to bet my combat pay. And I bet the third partner drives a dark blue sedan. I've seen it on the street, just hanging out. Kate saw it at the diner. We thought it belonged to the killer who was hunting her." Murph looked toward the road. "Do you know what this street is?"

Bing followed his gaze. Then he gave a quick grin.

"The shortcut between the bank and Route 1. For a quick getaway. They were scouting out their escape route, looking for traffic patterns." He reached for his radio unit. "Let's see if we have enough for a search warrant. I'm calling this in."

CHAPTER TWENTY-FIVE

Since Murph was driving down the interstate when his phone rang, Kate picked it up for him, blinking sleep from her eyes as she checked the display. "Captain Bing."

"Put him on speaker."

"Hey. Quick update," the captain said. "We have Wendy in custody, and we're searching for her two accomplices."

Kate and Murph had been removed from the property by the time the FBI stormed Wendy White's house, with local police assistance.

"Looks like you're going to receive some serious reward money for leading the authorities to the bank robbers," the captain went on. "Like a hundred grand."

Murph whistled. "So they did the hits, confirmed?"

"We found some marked bills from the last job at the house. Thought you'd want to know."

"Appreciate it. Thanks."

"Stay safe and come back soon."

"The second the FBI nips Asael's ass," Murph promised the man.

By the time they hung up, Kate was dancing in her seat.

"You're getting a reward!"

"We are getting a reward. We are engaged."

"I couldn't—I... We're just pretending we're engaged."

"I'm spending the first couple of hundred bucks on lingerie. I want to see you in black lace."

The heat in his eyes stole her breath. Obviously, they weren't going to be pretending *everything.*

Her mind immediately supplied a slew of images of all the things they would be doing for real. She resisted asking *Are we there yet?* But just barely.

She needed a distraction.

"Do you think Asael will try to find us?" She asked the question she knew would sober her in a second.

"He might not. Beyond anything else, he's smart. He's on the top of his game, uncaptured, which means he's smarter than the rest. He just saw his lover fail. He might realize that this is one situation he's better off staying away from. He has to know he'll be expected."

"Or he could want revenge badly enough not to give a flying fudge." She narrowed her eyes. "Are you trying to make me not worry?"

"You deserve to relax a little. When we get where we're going, I'll be giving you long speeches on a regular basis about always being prepared and all that. You can call me Drill Sergeant Dolan."

"I'm sure I'll be able to think of a number of names to call you." She smiled sweetly.

"So you do think he'll come after us?" she asked again after a minute, unable to let the subject drop.

"Probably, yes. Doesn't mean he'll find us."

"But if he does, we'll stand up to him together."

"Personal bodyguard on duty." He grinned. "And you'll be receiving extensive firearms training, martial arts all the way to black-belt level, and some other things. I have a list."

He might have been a tad overestimating what she was

capable of. "Is all that necessary?"

"Maybe not." He winked at her, in a lighter mood than she'd ever seen him. "Maybe it's just my fantasy to hook up with a hot special ops chick."

"Don't let me hold you back. Maybe you can meet one at the local VFW," she suggested as they passed the WELCOME TO OHIO sign.

"So funny. Do you need to stop at the next rest stop?"

"I'm good. How much farther?"

"We're about halfway there."

The Marshals Service had a house ready for them in eastern Ohio. Their new papers and new identities would be waiting for them at the house when they arrived. Murph and Kate had declined an escort.

She turned so she could fully look at him. "I still can't believe that you're coming with me. Broslin is your hometown. You have your house to finish. You could have gone back to the police department when your shoulder was better."

"I'll be fine. I'm right where I want to be."

He sounded gratifyingly sure, but she couldn't keep herself from pushing. "In Ohio?"

"With the woman I'm falling for." He looked at her. "Is that too fast?"

Her heart tripped. She felt his hot gaze on her skin as if he'd touched her. "I have no idea. I've never been in love before. I never trusted anyone enough. I don't know if I can."

"Same here. But I'm willing to give it a try."

So was she. "We could be terrible at this."

"Or we could learn to trust and figure things out as we go. I'd like to do that."

Her heart swelled. "Me too." If anyone was worth the risk, it was Murph.

A few seconds of silence stretched between them, too many thoughts crowding into her mind all at once, and some doubts as well. *Stupid.* She knew the kind of man

Murph was. This was a good card. And she was scared to pick up her ace because of all the bad cards she'd been dealt in the past. Maybe some part of her still didn't believe she deserved better.

Well, she did, dammit.

For a second, she thought of her mother and that long-ago lesson about cards. She thought of her family. Even if they couldn't be together right now, gratitude filled her heart. She was grateful for them, and for Murph.

"We'll be fine," she told him, her voice as sure now as his had been.

He flashed a sexy smile at her, full of desire and promise, that left her dazed for a second.

"I hate him. Mordocai," she said after a while. "He had to know I'd miss my dad. He pretended to be a father figure so I'd let my guard down around him."

"He was smart. But not smart enough. He's dead, and we're alive."

They came to a toll booth, a couple of cars in front of them. Looked like the guy at the gate had trouble finding enough change.

Murph unsnapped her seat belt and tugged her over, snuggled her to him. "I could have lost you."

"You didn't."

He kissed her.

He had amazing lips, and he knew how to use them. His warmth and strength enveloped her. As he deepened the kiss, desire shot through her, zipping all the way to her core.

The small sound of capitulation that escaped the back of her throat was answered by a feral growl.

They didn't realize the line of cars had started moving until someone beeped their horn behind them.

Kate scooted back to her side, snapped her seat belt on, her entire body flushed with heat.

Murph cleared his throat as he pulled forward and paid the toll, then stepped on the gas. "Maybe we should stop at the next rest stop. We've been on the road a while. We could take a break."

"We could get a hotel room and catch a quick nap," she suggested, oh so innocently.

His lips stretched into a grin. "We don't have to be *that* quick. At one point, I'd like to take my time with you, Miss Milano."

Katie Milano was her new identity. They were going into witness protection as an engaged couple. His new last name was Andrews. Their US Marshal contact had told them it meant "warrior" in Greek, so even Murph was pleased with the choice.

Tingles of anticipation raced across Kate's skin as she watched the smile that played about his masculine lips. She missed her family, but being with Murph felt right too. As if she belonged with him. She wished she could take him home to meet her parents and Emma. They would like Murph. *Maybe someday…*

"Do you think we'll ever be able to return to our real lives?" she asked.

"Yes."

"How do you know?"

"Robin said."

"The mail woman?" She narrowed her eyes. "Is she really psychic? She told you about the thresher, right? She predicted it?"

He shrugged. "Not exactly. Turns out she saw the thresher go into the barn when she was out walking her poodle."

"When was this?"

"The night Wendy came over with the cookies and had that infernal music playing with the volume turned up high."

So they wouldn't hear the engine rumble. Sneaky. And it'd been snowing, so the tire tracks were covered by morning. Kate shook her head, then changed the subject to something she'd been thinking about. "Do you think I should tell my family that I'm alive?"

She'd already asked Cirelli, and the agent had categorically said no, but the thought was impossible to set aside.

"No. There's a slim chance that Asael still doesn't know. Mordocai could have tracked you down on his own. He might have planned taking you out as a surprise present to his lover. Until Asael is in custody or dead, it'd be best to keep everything as it is right now."

"You think the FBI will catch him?"

"The agents have new leads now. Mordocai's DNA, for one. They'll be able to track him back to the odd jobs he did with Asael. Those hits will lead to new clues. This is the biggest break the FBI and Interpol ever had in the case."

"Okay." It wasn't as if the time they spent waiting would be terrible. She'd be with Murph. Kate smiled at him.

They drove over some potholes, and the blanket slid off their pile of boxes on the backseat. She reached out to straighten it, but not before Murph glanced at the rear-view mirror. His eyes narrowed.

"Is that the hot chocolate machine?"

"I'm bringing it."

"We talked about this."

"I never even got to try it."

"It's a gift from another man."

"You're jealous."

He harrumphed. "Maybe."

"We'll negotiate."

He drew up an eyebrow. "You're going to have to be awfully convincing." The sexual undertone in his voice sent tingles across her skin. The smoldering look in his eyes made her mouth go dry.

He flipped on his turn signal and took the next exit toward the Best Western that stood at the rise of the hill, the sun coming up behind the building.

Kate shifted on her seat, impatient to reach it.

* * *

Hot water sluiced down Murph's back, his hands

slippery with soap as he glided them over Kate's body. Food, shower, nap was the order of business they'd agreed on, on their way to the hotel. They were smack dab in the middle of their agenda.

"Isn't bathroom sex twice in the same day kind of decadent?" Kate asked weakly as he massaged his fingers over her nipples.

"I don't believe in quotas." He pinched each nipple and didn't let go, kept on the pressure.

He was determined to explore every inch of her body and test her responses, and smiled when she arched back, her eyelids drifting down. He liked to think she was powerless to resist.

Her exposed neck drew him, so he bent forward and scraped his teeth against her soft skin.

He let the pressure off her nipples. She gasped. He rolled the engorged nipples between his fingers, then pinched them again. Her breasts were incredibly sensitive and responsive. He could play with them for days.

The water washed away the soap, giving his fingertips more traction. She moaned.

He nipped her neck, then moved up to claim her lips.

As he ravaged her mouth, he released her nipples once again, his left hand rapidly sliding to her hip to anchor her, his right hand trailing a slower path to the patch of hair between her legs. In the same movement, without stopping, without hesitation, he slipped two fingers into her ready opening.

Her hands gripped his shoulders. "Murph!"

She sounded pained, so he stopped. But then she said "More" instead of protesting, and pushed her body against his hand, seeking, begging.

More sounded good to him. He was as hard as a police baton. But he wasn't going to rush this time. He bent his head to draw on one nipple first, then the other. Over and over again.

When she trembled, he withdrew his fingers from

inside her and got busy with her clitoris. He couldn't choose which part of her he liked the most.

She jerked against his hand.

His erection twitched between them.

Ladies first.

He massaged her swollen nub, returning his lips to her mouth again.

When at last she fell apart in his arms, he swallowed her cry of pleasure.

At the edge of his control, he scooped her up and strode to the bed with her, depositing her in the middle.

"We'll get the bedding wet," she said, breathless, her eyes glazed.

"I'll leave a big tip."

He reached for his shaving kit, grabbed a condom and slipped on protection. He nudged her knees up and apart. His entire body strained to be inside her, so he positioned the tip of his erection and pushed into her heat, into tight pleasure, all the way, grinding himself into her as her back bowed off the bed and her fingers gripped the sheets.

He held still. If he moved even a little…

She squirmed. *Ahh.* But he waited, with superhuman strength, until he gained some semblance of control. Only then did he begin to move. Very carefully.

Take it slow. Take it slow. Take it slow! But too soon, on its own, his body picked up speed.

"Murph," she begged. "Harder. I won't break. Please."

To hell with holding back. He pounded into her, her body convulsing around him all of a sudden, gripping him like a fist. And that was the end of him.

When he was spent, he held on to her and rolled them so she'd be on top. He had to work to catch his breath.

She snuggled against him and kissed the line of his jaw. "I could get used to this."

This was it. She was it for him, he thought with crystal-clear clarity. He was never going to let go of her. *Never.*

* * *

Murph Dolan had officially blown her mind. And captured her heart. And wrung out her body. Kate stayed sprawled on top of him, not just because she liked the feeling, but because she couldn't have moved for a trunkful of chocolate.

She listened to his heart slow little by little as it returned to a steady rhythm. She felt content, happy, and safe.

Long minutes passed before she finally raised her head to look at him. How on earth had he gotten to her so fast? She furrowed her brow.

Maybe he interpreted that as worry, because he said, "We'll be fine once we settle into our new lives."

"I know. How long do you think we'll be gone?"

"Not long. Like I said, the FBI is closer to Asael than they've ever been before. They'll grab him, then we come home, and everything will be back to normal."

"Didn't Bing hire Jack Sullivan to fill your job?"

"Temporarily."

"I have this *feeling* about him."

Murph raised an eyebrow.

"Not like that." She fought back a grin. "Not like a premonition even, just… He's deep, dark waters."

"Now you sound like Robin."

"I wish. If I could forecast the future…"

"You'd see us naked. Together. A lot."

That made her laugh. She was sooo ready for the future Murph painted.

But then his expression clouded, and he added, "I'm probably not done with the nightmares. There could be all kinds of weirdness coming out post-deployment. That's what they tell you at the hospital. If we'll be living together long-term… I just thought you should know. But I'm going to handle it."

Chocolate had always been her favorite word, but *long-term* sounded pretty fantastic too, Kate decided. "Okay."

"Just like that?"

"Nobody's perfect. I'm a chocoholic."

"It's not exactly the same."

"We make a pretty good team."

He smiled. "We do. You know what they say. *Home is where the heart is.*"

"You're a soldier and a police officer, a warrior and all that involves. Why do you get to be wise too?" She gave a mock frown. "What do I get to be?"

"Smart, sexy and crazy about me." He grinned at her. "What do you have to say about that?"

She smiled back, her heart filled with warmth. "I'm not going to argue with anything that starts with me being smart and sexy."

The End

(OK, not really. Murph and Kate will be returning to Broslin in a future novel, DEATHTOLL, so you'll see them again. Right now, however… Ready for handsome Jack Sullivan and his secrets? Meet the tortured hero and the reclusive Broslin artist who steals his heart. Next book: **DEATHSCAPE. #1 Amazon Romantic Suspense Bestseller**)

"Spine-chilling suspense that will leave you on the edge of your seat." (The Romance Reviews, DEATHSCAPE)

Thank you for reading my books! To be notified when my next title comes out, please sign up for my **New Book Alerts** on my web site (danamarton.com). I send out a one-page note, once a month tops (and sometimes not even that frequently), so I promise not to overwhelm your email! I also always notify my readers of upcoming sales and giveaways.

Wishing you all the best,
Dana Marton
Author

Broslin Creek books by Dana Marton

DEATHWATCH…..(Book 1)
DEATHSCAPE……(Book 2)
DEATHTRAP……..(Book 3)
DEATHBLOW……(Book 4)
BROSLIN BRIDE…(Book 5)
DEATHWISH……..(Book 6)
DEATHMARCH…..(Book 7)
DEATHTOLL……..(Book 8)

www.ingramcontent.com/pod-product-compliance
Lightning Source LLC
La Vergne TN
LVHW021925070725
815537LV00009B/604

* 9 7 8 1 9 4 0 6 2 7 0 0 7 *